THE GENTLE GIANT RETURNS

Crime, Thriller, Mystery

By M.L. Weatherington

The Gentle Giant Returns
ISBN-13: 978-1-942622-18-5

This book edition is published by: Pynhavyn Press First Edition: September ,2018 http://www.pynhavyn.com

Acknowledgements

Normally I keep a log of all that happens during the writing of my novels and thereby I have the dates and names of people who have helped me move forward with my writing. This time was so different. I wrote and while I did life happened. Among which I moved, into a smaller home. I down sized in more ways than one. I did not keep notes as I went along. So, my thanks must be all encompassing.

I appreciate each and everyone who helped me make this book a success. I just can't put names down without worrying that I have missed someone. I don't want to do that. You have all encouraged me and I have grown from all the input.

To my old friends...thank you, thank you so much.

To my new friends, those I have made this year, thank you for becoming my fan. I hope you will stay for a long time.

Mary

Jeremiah 20:11

For I know the plans I
have for you, declares the
LORD, plans for welfare
and not evil, to give you a
future and a hope.

Chapter One

4: 30 p.m. October 14, 1995

Summer seemed lazy this Saturday, stretching its warm fingers into October's afternoon. A gentle breeze carried the floral fragrances to the little table. It couldn't have been better arranged.

Just as Art lifted the almost empty bottle, Doctor Jim Wexford strolled across the distance from the house to where Amanda and Art sat. "I hate to break up this little party but..."

They both turned to him with smiles plastered on their faces, the wine in their glasses almost gone.

"Any chance I can empty that bottle for you?"

Art peered at Amanda and with his eyes gave her a questioning look that asked, "Shall we share?"

A twinkle sparkled in her eye as she nodded, and Art lifted the bottle, "It's almost gone, Jim. You might get a swallow." Art drained the container as the doc opened the wooden folding chair he carried along with the wine goblet.

He took the wine glass with the golden liquid rolling around the bottom and upended it in one smooth move, "Awe, this is good." Jim brought the goblet down and as he sat said, "Let me see the label."

Art turned the bottle, and the doc nodded. "Made right here in Lodi."

Art stretched his legs out and looked at Doc Wexford. He knew this man didn't jump in where he probably wasn't needed for just any reason. He appraised the doc and waited. Then thought, *He's here about Stumper.* "I talked to Walt, and they've got Stumper solid on murder charges. He's going to the Grand Jury.

"Why did he kill that woman?"

"Well," Art looked at Amanda and could see she was all ears. "It seems that the ex, Adora, was artful at bleeding him dry. He felt he had nothing more to give and she was after even that."

"So, he just got rid of his problem." The doc lifted his glass again to drink but realized that it was empty, and he set it on the table. He looked at Amanda and could see how happy she was, and he smiled. "I am glad you two found your way back to each other."

"So are we," they chimed in at the same time, and then the three laughed. Out of friendship, the three sat in the warmth that was soon to pass into a cold hard winter that Lodi would not forget, and the weather channel would allude to on other occasions. Right now, they relaxed in the doc's garden area of an extensive well-manicured grounds surrounding a centuries-old fashionable structure, it's exterior a delight to study with its turned wooden embellishments. It had seen better days and the exterior needed paint bad, but that was coming as soon as the inside had its overhaul, Jim had told Art.

"You miss Stumper?"

"Do I. He was a worker." The doc shook his head. "I can do the work, but its help with the heavy lifting stuff or the long beams. I will find someone else, just hope he is as good as Stumper." The doc looked at Art a long moment, and the breeze streamed through the feathery redwood leaves on thick limbs high above them. "What about the person that had you in their sights. Is that over?"

Art shot his eyes to the docs, and they locked. There was a deeper meaning to this question Art knew. After a long moment, he understood. He said, "You are worried about Amanda. She safe with me?"

Jim nodded. "She's my friend, and I don't want to see anything happen to her. You could be a dangerous guy to connect up with. I really don't know you all that well. No offense intended."

"None taken." Art looked at Amanda she was very interested in his answer, and he wanted to say just the right things to make them realize that he was safe from that attack and that he would not involve her in anything dangerous. He knew that he was not going to be in law enforcement as a means of earning a living. His arm was going to be the reason for that switch in life. Although the idea simmered somewhere in the back of his mind, he still wanted to return to the department–His answer came from that point of view. "I think the man who shot at me didn't want to kill me. He was making a statement with his wife who wanted me dead for taking the life of her grandson. I know it sounds awful. McNamare will be yesterday's news and remain history."

"Is he going to jail?"

"Well, he didn't kill anyone."

"He's going free?" Amanda sat forward her eyes wide with concern.

Art shook his head to make her feel there was nothing to worry about. "He'll be in the court system, might have to go through therapy."

"Is that all?"

"Time will tell." He wanted to get them off this subject since he didn't know what the legal outcome would be. He'd looked in the man's eyes the day that he caught him and was aware that it was over, and he was safe from him coming after him in the future. *How do you explain that to these two?* "Well, you didn't just get out here to see how Amanda and I were doing. Or to have a glass of wine. So, what's up?"

"You can't wait, can you? You've got your nose to the ground. What is it with you, a scent of crime or something else that gets your juices going?"

Art smiled and waited. He looked at Amanda and could see she was interested in his answer to that question. He laughed, "Guess I'll let you figure it out on your own."

The doc rubbed his palms together. "Remember a few days ago, before you left for Florida, I called and asked you to come over, that I had found something and wanted to show it to you.?"

"Yes."

The doc stood and pointed toward the house. "It's in the house, can you come now?"

"Both of us?"

"Sure."

They walked away from the little peach colored table, the ends of the cloth swaying in the slight breeze. It pleased Art, the walking together across the lush lawn neatly trimmed and edged with his friend and Amanda.

"Maybe this is nothing, but I thought you might have some thoughts on what's down there and I should run it past you before I tear it all out in my demolition."

Harsh clopping sounds echoed as they walked across the wooden porch and the Doc opened the front door. "Watch your step. There are building supplies everywhere."

Art took Amanda's hand, and she trailed him as he followed the doc. They went through the living area and the dining area, dodging boxes and tools and one humongous ladder. Finally, the doc opened a door, and they approached stairs going down a long narrow passage. It smelled musty and made Art want fresh air, but they kept going down until they were on the floor.

"It's dirt?"

"Yes."

"A lovely house like this and the basement is dirt floor?"

"I was surprised too when I first came down here. It's over here."

They followed him to the back wall, and they looked at some chains that were attached to the wall. They had cuffs at the end, and it gave Art chills when he saw them.

"Someone was held down here?"

"That's what it looks like to me too. But then I found this."

They trailed the doc to the end of the wall. He opened another door and before them lay another set of stairs. These were cut out of the dirt, and the side walls pressed in on Art as he moved down the twenty steps to an area where you could not stand full height. They were well underground at this point, and Jim held a flashlight to illuminate the area. The spot of light moved lazily across the wall then downward and came to a stop. "What do you make of that?

Chapter Two

The chill of the damp walls got to Art's arm, and the scent of dirt tickled his nose. The thought of sneezing passed his mind as he shook off the cold. The arm sling seemed more in the way right now than helpful to him. Art wrapped his fingers around the shoulder strap. He lifted and adjusted it. No help. The throb still pulsated through him like a speaker with the base turned up full blast. He didn't want to be a wuss and let them know how much this place made his arm ache, or him uncomfortable, so he gritted his teeth. "Jim, how many times have you come down here?"

Jim's dark eyes darted off to the side as he thought. The Light from his flashlight danced as he spoke. "Just that once. It gave me that uneasy feeling when something is wrong, so I backed out of here and called you." He coughed and cleared his throat while brushing the dust off his shoulder.

"I am wondering how this could be? I mean, it's so far underground."

"Best I can tell you, this place was added onto over the years. It was big and grand to start with but made more magnificent by each generation. There's some residual proof of water damage, probably the river crested and flooded to this house. The original house was lower, and a stable was about here. That's according to the plans I have. I think they rebuilt shortly after the turn of the century. And they brought in the dirt and built the land against the future water's rise. I believe that it tore the land away leaving a cliff and they, at some point did their best to back the river off. I think the river was handled by the town folk to keep the floods from damaging all of Lodi. Then dirt was brought in, and they reclaimed the land. What I've been able to learn about this old place suggests that a lot of Japanese came here to work and to start a business. It looks like one of the families owned this property and they were flooded out. That was in the 1800's."

Amanda leaned into to Art. She trembled, and it stoked him that she would look to him for protection. The excitement unnerved him. As did the emerald silk blouse as his hand slid down the curve of her back. He loved everything about her, causing him to call upon his cop training as he wrapped his arm around her soft body, cuddling her close to his. Maybe she's cold. He sank his chin into the silky blonde hair near her ear and smelled the lavender shampoo she'd used. "Are you cold?"

Amanda shook her head and snuggled closer. "It's creepy. What do you think of those chains?"

He raised his chin and turned more toward Jim. "What do you think?"

"I think history will show that they were used for slavery, to keep someone from leaving. They are old, homemade, probably hammered out by a blacksmith."

Art nodded, "Yeah, I don't think they have anything to do with current events. You didn't go poking around?"

The doc moved the flashlight beam around the walls and ceiling to show them the whole area. "No." His beam momentarily lit Art's red hair and mustache, a sharp contrast to the darkness of the basement.

Art nodded, "Come on let's get out of here. By the looks of it, this is a crime scene, and we don't want to muck it up and lose any of the clues."

The three turned and started back up the steps, brushing the dirt walls as they climbed. Each stair seemed off level and about a four-inch rise making it a bit difficult to get a sound footing, but finally, they were back in the basement on the dirt floor. Art reached over and took the flashlight from Jim. "Just follow right behind me."

"What do you think happened down here?" Amanda said.

"Jim, when did you make the find?"

"I told you. When I called you and asked you to come? So, what...ten days or so. Why?"

"We need to call Walt and get him over here." Satisfied that he had seen everything down in the basement, he handed the flashlight back. "The guys are going to be working this house for some time. Go upstairs and put a bag together for your needs. Take some clothes. Amanda and I will witness what you take."

The doc stiffened, apparently ready to protest, "Is that necessary?"

"You don't want to be here while the police are working. Take my word for it."

They made their way back to the dining area, closing the door to the basement.

"You think that's a grave down there?" Amanda said.

"Graves." Art said.

"Oh God, what went on here?" Jim shook his head, resting his right hand on the ladder.

"I don't know Jim, but the department needs to get over here now." Art moved around on the right side of the tall ladder, pushing gently on Amanda's shoulder, wanting to make sure she was safely out of there. He knew the three would be answering questions and the sooner they got that over with, the better.

"Can I use your phone, Jim?"

"Sure, there's one in the kitchen on the wall."

Art and Amanda followed the doc into the kitchen, and Art went right to the phone. "Walt," he said after a long moment.

"Art."

"I need you to come over to Doc Wexford's place right now. There's a suspicious scene here."

Art took the receiver from his ear and turned toward Amanda and Jim. "Walt said he'd be here in fifteen minutes." Art replaced the phone and looked at them. Amanda and Jim had similar expressions of wonder and curiosity written all over their faces. "Just what you needed. A hold up on your demolition."

The doc's eyes went wide, "How long do you think that's going to be?"

"As long as it takes, so if I know Walt, we don't have a lot of time to get your stuff out of here. He's going to close this place down."

"What!" The doc took a step toward Art.

"Suck it up, Jim. This is out of your control from here on out. You did right calling me."

Jim's shoulders dropped and he nodded.

The three headed for the stairway up to the second floor. "My bedroom's this way." They climbed the stairs, their hands caressing the oak banister. Art noticed a smell, not unpleasant but one that said ancient. The maroon carpet muffled their footsteps and gave Art the sense of being in a stately mansion. History was reaching off the walls, feeding his imagination of those times and events. Candle holders positioned head high made him grin. *Imagine having nothing but flickering illumination you have to put a flame to each evening. I flip the switch without thinking.* His finger tapped one of the candle receptacles, "I bet they went to bed early in those days. Hey, Jim. When did this house get electricity?"

"That's an excellent question. I know it has nob and tube because I found it inside the walls downstairs. The main part of the house has been upgraded, probably after 1950's. It needs it again."

"Nob and tube not proper wiring?"

"No, it's perfectly safe, and cheaper by about a third. Code calls for something else these days."

"If these walls could talk," Amanda said as she wrapped her hand around the jamb and turned into the room. "These quarters are small by today's building standards. Character screamed from the first minute I entered this house. Oh Jim, this place is going to be beautiful when you are through."

Jim's bed had a comforter in shades of blue draped over the sheets and mattress. Wild roses rambled over the walls and, at some point, the woodwork in oak must have shone with high luster. A chair placed by the bed had an electric clock sitting on its seat. A large framed painting stared down from the north wall, and an old dresser waited on the east wall.

The three of them stood shoulder to shoulder, Jim the tallest and Art stair-stepping down to Amanda. After a pause, Jim strode across the floor and went right to work.

Art watched him remove a suitcase from under the bed and open the drawer of an old antique dresser. He removed underwear and socks. The top drawer had some handkerchiefs. Jim took six and placed them in the suitcase. There were some knit T-shirts in the third drawer down, and he chose four of them.

The Doc turned to Art. "You say this is going to take a long time, that I can't get into the house, even to work?"

Art, a grimace on his face, nodded. "Take as much as you think you will need. It could be a long time before you get back into this room."

Amanda stepped over by the window and ran her hand over the wall, "Look at the old roses on this paper. Isn't it a lovely design?"

"Glad you like them cause they're pretty much out of here when I demo," Doc chimed in as he gathered some toiletries. From the armoire, he chose some shirts and pants. Amanda held out her hands and Jim gave the hanging shirts to her. He carried his bag and pants. "That's it for now."

"Okay, let's get out on the porch and wait for Walt."

They walked to the landing and looked over, "Boy, they lived grandly didn't they."

Amanda slid in between the men, the hanging shirts held by her crooked finger off her shoulder. She pointed with her other hand. "I can just see the Christmas tree over there by the window. A big one going to the ceiling."

Art looked at the spot she mentioned. It was to the right of the massive brick fireplace. Thick window sills and window trimmings of oak wood framed the small panes of old glass. He could imagine the tree as she spoke. *She has the heart of a poet.* "I wonder if they put candles on the tree?"

She said, "Can you imagine cutting down a tree that big and getting it through that doorway?"

Art swung his attention to the front entry, "Oh, I think you could get one in that opening. The access is bigger than usual. That's a custom door, isn't it?" He glanced at the doc.

"Yeah, it is. That's one of the things I just love about this house. It's different than most homes in the area. I know it's going to be a job getting it restored, but I am going to do my best."

Art's eyes closed and he smiled. As he opened them, he saw all the building supplies and tools stored in the first-floor living and dining area, recognizing all the work still to be done. For him, it chased the illusion of Christmas and happier times away. "Let's get outside and meet Walt on the front porch."

The three worked their way down the stairs and past all the clutter to the front door. It creaked as Jim opened it. A strong scent of pine met Art as they moved over the wooden porch to the railing. There they placed the clothing and the bag beside them and strolled listlessly to the wicker chairs and sat. Amanda crossed her ankles and rubbed her knees. Their eyes met. Quietly they waited, the gentle breeze picking up and cooling the shaded porch. Jim's kind face held a worried look giving his wrinkles more profound definition, the usual peaceful expression in his eyes replaced by concern. Art moved his mustache in little jerks, showing his uneasiness. The frustration brought on by his not being in charge, and his sincere desire to be in control. Amanda let a smile come and go on her lips as though she could not make up her mind how she felt.

Finally, the white car Walt drove came to a stop.

The three made sounds with the movement of their bodies and sighs as they acknowledged his arrival and waited for Walt to reach the porch.

Walt, his white shirt stuffed into his black pants, shuffled past the pine trees sheltering the walk. He climbed the stairs. His eyes focused on all Jim's packed clothing, staying on them for quite a long moment. With lips pressed firmly together as though making a deep discernment, he turned to Art, Amanda, and Jim. "It's that bad?"

Chapter Three

Art followed Walt's fliting eyes as he studied the wooden porch and the packed bags huddled near the steps where the detective stood. Art figured he was finished looking around, and he was right, as Walt nodded. Art raised himself and joined him. Without words, their footsteps announced their movement toward the front door. A sharp crack sounded as the large entry door suction broke free. As it opened, it added a degree of creepiness to this already odd-ball investigation.

Just before walking in Art glanced back at Amanda and by the look of her, he knew fear held her in its grip. She sat forward in a wicker chair with her elbows on her knees, her fingers intertwined and her chin rested on top of them. Her wide eyes added to the worried expression that bloomed on her face.

She should be used to police work after working with the department all these years. Maybe she's just not been this close to the crime scene before. This kind of police work must be new to her. Her work was always after the fact. I'll have to talk to her later.

"This way Walt." They made their way through the living room and dining room to the stairwell. Art watched Walt take in every detail: the open box of hand tools, the ladder, boxes stacked against one wall. Art opened the door leading to the basement and backed away, so Walt could check it out. Walt looked down the old rickety wooden stairs. He looked back at Art and indicated he should go first. A coolness enclosed them as Art began.

"What do you think is down here?"

"At least three graves. Maybe more." Art's voice echoed as it bounced off the dirt.

"Crud!"

"My thoughts exactly."

The cold rushed them as they made the first couple of steps. The darkness oozed over them. "It's tight going," Art said, using his healthy arm to press against the wall of the stairwell and hold Jim's flashlight that darted around like a firefly. Walt turned his light on. It had a much stronger beam that haloed like a spotlight on a stage floor seeking a diva. They stepped off the last step and found themselves on a dirt floor. Art pointed out the chains and cuffs.

Walt moved closer to them. "These are not new."

"Right."

Walt leaned down and picked one cuff up. "When was this house built?"

"Well, I'd say before the turn of the century. Eighteen something."

He let the chain clank back into place, scraping the wall as it swung to a stop. "What was going on down here?"

"Come over here." Art walked over to the other door that led down to the lower basement area. "The going is slow here. Smell that musty odor?"

"Yeah."

They moved down into the lower basement and stood side by side, running the beams of light over the entire area. The walls were rough and hacked to shape the space. Like someone was in a hurry. "It must have taken a lot of time to get all this dirt out. Someone had to carry it out bucket by bucket." He looked at Walt's face and smiled. "Thing of it is, it just doesn't look new to me. I think it's been a long time since anything was happening down here."

Walt scratched his ear. "I'm just thinking about the process that would be needed to work this place. I'm going to bring a couple of guys from our department."

"I'm going to get the guys over here and get started. Cause this site just might solve some cold cases."

Walt reached into his pocket and pulled out a wrapped piece of hard candy. He worked it in his one hand trying to unwrap it, but it would not open. At last, he bit at the twisted end, the candy slipped free, and Walt popped the morsel into his mouth. He made a humming noise in answer to Art's question, crumpled the paper up and shoved it in his pocket.

"I knew you would. There may be all kinds of evidence down here." Art moved toward the mounds. "Amanda and I watched Jim put his things together. He took only his clothing and some toilet items. He's ready to go."

"That certainly looks like a grave."

Art moved his light beam, "There are two more."

"Un-huh." Walt huffed. "Good, good. I'll get the team assembled and over here this afternoon. Boy, Lodi's been a quiet little town with a low crime rate. Lately, it seems to be busting at the seams, what with what happened to you last July. How's the arm coming?"

15

Art looked at Walt and realized he hadn't thought about his arm much since he got back from Florida. A private grin cracked his lips. He didn't want to tell Walt everything that was going on in his life. The information about him and Amanda didn't need to be spread all over the department. Not yet anyway. He looked down at his arm and answered, "It's not been so bad lately, better than a month ago. Maybe it's getting better."

Walt gazed at the three mounds, "Good, then you can come back and take this one. I don't like being down here one bit. This place is going to get my arthritis acting up. It's cold, bone aching damp, and eerie. It's like being in a grave."

"I'd like to. Have you seen enough?"

"Like to what?"

"Come back to work."

"Yep, let's get out of here."

They made their way back up to the dirt floor. Walt took one last look at the stairs going down, and he shook his head. "Those are a bitch. When did the doc move in?"

"That's a question we need to answer. He is the one that brought this to my attention. He had called me before I went to Florida."

"Yeah, how'd that go?"

"Well, I sent my only daughter, Melissa, with her mother Evelyn, a woman my baby girl had never met before Mel's sixteenth birthday, to Florida. As soon as Murph and I took McNamare down and I knew that it was safe for Melissa to come back, I went and got her. I didn't want Evelyn to get any fancy ideas."

"Un-huh."

"What do you mean, un-huh?"

"No chance for you and Evelyn to get together?" Walt turned to Art, waiting for his answer.

Art looked him straight in the eye and shook his head, his face stern, his mustache set and firm. "Not a chance. That boat has sailed."

Walt shrugged his shoulders, "She seemed a lovely lady."

They started for the door again.

"It wasn't the right match years ago, and it's not the right match now."

"Just saying. Maybe Melissa would like to have her mother closer."

"I know she would. You haven't seen her since we got home have you?"

Walt stopped moving toward the door and turned to Art, "No, why?"

"She's got her hair cut off. At first, I didn't know what I thought. It was a shock. And I do miss the hair and seeing it swing when she turned around. There was a sound that went with the movement, and I miss that. But I must admit she is growing up, and it fits her. Come by. We'll have dinner and you can see her." Art looked down and then off to the far wall of the basement. Some narrow windows let defused light past massive cobwebs. Old shelves, sagging now, lined the west wall. It seemed to Art that home canned foods probably sat on those shelves, in the 1900's. This place was one of the first big homes built here, he thought. He also believed that the house held a mystery, one it would not give up easily.

The basement walls now covered with peeling shiplap were clear of most everything but pipes. *Jim's probably going to upgrade the whole place, and all this will be gone.* He came back to the moment at hand and looked at Walt. "The guys will have to go through this place first."

Walt nodded, and they headed for the stairs to the dining area.

Back outside they met Jim and Amanda who stood as soon as they came out of the house.

"What do you think?"

"Well, Jim, we think it's a crime scene and the department will be going over this place for evidence starting this afternoon. So, you can come live with Melissa and me for the time being."

Jim looked down at his shoes and shook his head. "It's a crime scene?"

"Afraid so Jim."

"I'll carry the shirts," Amanda offered.

Each one took something, and Jim locked the front door and held the key out.

Walt's chubby hand circled around the key, and Jim gave it to him. "I'll need you all to come down to the station to make a statement. Later today if possible."

Jim nodded and made his way to the car where he placed his bag and the other clothing he took from Art and Amanda. He turned, looked at the different faces and then at his house. It was standing elegantly on the property, displaying its age and craftsmanship while at the same time hiding all its secrets. He'd grown fond of the project and had such high hopes for its final reveal. Jim was planning to live here himself and finding love like Amanda and Art have found. He wasn't too old to start a family. He turned back to Walt, "I'll come down as soon as I can."

"Good. Art, I'll take you up on that dinner invitation, if Melissa is cooking," Walt said and waved two fingers in the air.

Art smiled. Don't like Cajun cooking?" He grinned at Walt, showing teeth.

Expertly Amanda caught the exchange between Walt and Art. "Who cooks Cajun?"

18

Art turned to Amanda, "He's eaten my food and calls it Cajun cooking because I burn things. Sometimes."

Walt turned on that remark. "Sometimes?" he said, grinning. "You have the fire department on call."

"Oh, it's not that bad." Art smiled and followed Walt to the car, reaching the unit by the front fender. He lowered his voice, "What's your first move?"

Walt gave him his full attention. "I'm going to get the history on this place from county records and see what crime records I can pull up from our end. I'll get Tracy working on it today when I get back."

Art nodded. "That's all good. Those chains in the wall, I think that's an old matter. I didn't notice any evidence of recent use near them." Art leaned his backside against the fender as he waited for Walt's reaction.

Walt bobbed his head, placing his focus on the ground. "I'll get started and we'll see what turns up." He sliced his eyes at Art, "I'm just hoping this isn't a serial killing site. I've heard of backyard graveyards before. Basements, now that's a new wrinkle."

Art let his head drop. "I really wish you hadn't said that."

Chapter Four

Aart's foot pressed the brake, and his hand went to the key and twisted until the car quieted. The softness of the afternoon sounded so different from town traffic. A breeze picked up and rustled the leaves over his head. Peace filled him, and for just a second, he let the reality settle in before his hand gripped the door handle. As he did a smile parted his lips, and a look of pleasure bloomed across his face. Today he wore a flannel shirt of plaid hues in dark blue, a pair of new denim jeans, a pair of brown slip-on shoes, and his green arm sling. He no longer worried about how he looked or what Amanda might think of his clothing choice. His feeling of reassurance had grown as they grew closer to each other.

Amanda stood with her back to him, looking out over the lake. The tall grass reeds rose from the water and stood like sentinels on guard. Lodi Lake was like glass at this time of day, mirroring the bank abundantly with colors of green, brown, and yellow splashed across the surface of the lake edge and contrasted strikingly with her body and hair. *How could such a creature be so lovely?*

She stood as though she didn't know he was there. Her hands were together behind her back and her fingers were wrapped around the picnic basket handle. She wore a skirt of crème toned checks and a pearl-white sweater. Her blonde hair almost completely covered the golden collar of her blouse. She exuded a confidence he admired. Here was a person who didn't need him, she wanted him.

Art recognized those old sturrings, his lips parted as his smile broadened and a twinkle sparkled from his eyes. She excited him in ways that Art had never imagined he would feel again. He pressed down on the handle, and the door opened. He stepped out, and his foot squashed down on dried leaves and made a noise she couldn't have missed. She did not turn to him. The car door clunked shut, and she stood like a statue. Art moved toward her, not trying to hide his approach. He could feel her smile and that she wanted to hide it from him. There was a comfort about their relationship, and it was growing every moment they were together. However, the re-connecting times were the most exclusive to Art. No. Exciting!

"Hi." Art's voice had a husky, raw tone.

"Hi," she answered and turned to him. Before he could say anything more, she reached to the tips of her toes and pressed her lips to his.

Art felt instant thrills race through him as her warmth pressed hard against his side and the stab of her knee into his leg made contact. It didn't matter. He loved the gentleness of her touch, the softness of her flesh, the moment their lips met. He closed his eyes and lingered with his neck bent to connect with her. He breathed, but he didn't know how or how much. It didn't matter. Only the two of them mattered. The moment moved slow and pleasurably and as they pulled apart their lip tissue clung as though they resisted the parting. His eyes were filled with her. Schoolboy looks covered Arts cheeks, and he let his teeth show as he smiled down at her. He felt so in love with her and so afraid that his feelings might show. He changed the subject. "What's in the basket?"

She brought the basket around her body, and they both looked into the interior as her hand moved the red checkered cloth covering the opening. "Well, there's a bottle of wine, some cheese and red apples."

"What kind of cheese?"

"I got a package of assorted flavors. There's a hot pepper cheese, and some jack cheese and sharp cheddar." Her hand pulled the wine out, and she said, "I went over to Snow White and got two bison burgers with everything on them."

Tucked under her right arm, Amanda held a blanket. She pulled it forward. Art took one end and watched as she set the basket down, and together they opened the blanket out and spread it on the ground.

He took her hand and helped her down. She smiled up at him as he dropped down to his knees and rolled to his hip to get down beside her. "This is nice. I didn't expect anything to eat when you called and asked me to meet you here." Art pawed through the basket hunting for the package of cheese, then brought it out and opened it. "Want some?"

"Not yet." She leaned back on her left arm and looked at his face.

It made him heat up inside, and he couldn't help but beam.

"I wanted to have a talk." She leaned closer to him. "I mean a real talk."

"About?"

"Well," she dropped her eyes and smoothed her skirt. Slowly they came back up and studied his. "I think we should clear the air about some things."

"Okay. What things?"

She looked around and over the surface of the lake, bringing her gaze back to him, "I want to know where I stand in all of it."

"All of what?" The smile faded, and his lips rested together softly yet firmly as he waited.

She looked at him with a serious expression. "Art. I want to know how all the players in your life fit together."

"Players?" The mustache twitched and the wrinkles deepened between his eyes bringing the eyebrows closer together. A hint of fear raced through his body. What are you getting at?

"Yes. How does Evelyn fit in?" She paused and sighed. "I guess I am asking if I get involved with you," Amanda's eyes had a dull look as she stared into his, "is she going to come back at some point? Will you want to marry her?"

His head went up and his eyes closed as a sense of 'I understand' was conveyed in that movement. "You don't have any worries in that department."

A little working of her lips showed her pleasure in his words. "Elaborate please."

Art wanted to reach over and draw her close and hug her, but his darn arm was in the way. Hanging there useless in the green sling, it trapped him. "Evelyn came to meet Melissa, and she instantly fell in love with her daughter. I didn't know she was coming. It was a complete surprise to me. She wanted to make a family and let that idea be known to Melissa and me."

"And me."

Art looked surprised. "Oh? How?"

"That morning that I came over. The one where I said goodbye at the curb. Evelyn was standing in your front window wearing only two bath towels. One was around her body and the other around her head. She had moved in and wanted me to understand she was in charge." A tear played in Amanda's eyes, showing passion and a quiver on her lips proved her emotional state. "I am a grown up. If we are not going to be together, I can live with that." Her voice lowered. "I don't want to."

Art recognized fear and wanted to take the feeling away. There would be a time to speak, but right now she needed to talk. He waited.

"I felt you needed to make up your mind between us. It's her or me. That simple. And, I need to hear from you that you are a one-woman man and will stick with whoever you choose."

He moved his bottom to be closer to her. A smile crossed his entire face, and he carefully chose his next words. "Amanda. You have my heart. You are my forever love. I can't imagine not being with you. The minute we are apart, I want to call you. See you. I've even driven to your office and sat in the car just looking at the closed door. I did that just to be near you. You were working so I didn't let myself barge in. But I wanted to." He shook his head for emphasis, "You don't know this about me Honey, but when I make a promise, I keep my promise." His fingers slipped closer to her leg, settling on the soft dark blue plaid blanket.

Her fingers found him, and they touched. "I am so glad to hear you say that. But there's one more thing. Melissa. What does she want? I would rather imagine she wants her mother in her life. Especially now that she's met her and spent time with her. Would she want me as a stepmom? This is all important. Art, you can't make a family. It just happens. And..."

"Amanda. Let me tell you something. When I went to Florida to get Mel, I didn't think we had a chance. You and me. I thought you wanted out. It about killed me, but

I was willing to let you go if that was your wish. It was Mel that told me her mom ran you off. She said she'd told her mother that you and I were going to marry and we'd be a family."

"Mel said that?"

"She did. You are her choice for mom."

Amanda's eyes drifted to his. "You've talked to her about me and you, my being her stepmom?"

Art nodded, dropped his eyes to the cheese package and smiled. "We had a long talk on the plane ride home. She chooses you because, and these are her words, "Mom makes you crazy, "meaning me. "And Amanda makes you happy. Mom would never be there, she'd always be flying off somewhere, and Amanda will be there. I want a mom that's there." Art watched her reaction, and it was exactly as he hoped it would be. "Then she said this, "'Amanda makes you happy, and I like seeing you happy dad.'"

Amanda took it all in and fought tears that wanted to come. Relief filled her, and it showed by her shoulders dropping and a smile that seemed warm and inviting. "I've been like a kid wanting to be near you, to come where you are, to call you. It's as if I am driven. I'm trained in the field of emotions. I can tell you, Art, these feelings are strong and demanding. Her fingers circled his, and she moved closer, her intention to kiss clearly shown in her actions. He started to meet her just as a duck quacked and startled them out of their feelings.

Art sat straight. "We are outside for all the world to see. Guess we should follow decorum and act our ages."

She threw her head back and laughed. As she turned her attention to Art, she said, "That's no fun, Art Franklin. No fun at all."

He picked up the wine bottle and looked in the basket for an opener. "An excellent red. Syrah."

Amanda's hand came up and tapped the bottle. "The bottle's aged nine years." Art nodded approval and said, "Did you know that these grapes are black?"

"No."

Art gripped the bottle with his bad arm, crushed it to his chest and pushed the corkscrew into the cork and pulled. The cork wouldn't budge.

"Here, give." She held her hand out and gripped the bottle around the neck. He let it go, and she easily pulled the cork free. "Art, don't. It's no big deal. Your arm is damaged and needs time. Give it time. Everything will work out. But for now, there are two glasses in the basket. Let's eat those juicy burgers before they get any colder."

A dark look covered his face as the disgust with his disabilities showed. He smiled a weak tweak of the lips and became serious in an instant. The glasses were easy to reach, and he handed them one at a time to her. She filled a glass for him, and he took it from her. "The smell is gorgeous."

Amanda looked around for a place to set her drink, but there seemed no place. She handed it to Art, and he held two plastic glasses in one hand while she brought the sandwiches from the basket. With ease, she unwrapped his and placed it on his lap using the wrapper as a plate. Then Amanda opened hers and took her glass back. Art raised his glass and sipped. "Oh, that's nice. Blueberries. Hm... peppery. Did you notice that?"

"Yes. It's strong. I'm going to need something to eat with it." Amanda bit into her sandwich, rustling the wrapper as she ate.

Art managed to settle his glass in a tilted position on the ground beside him, and he picked up his sandwich and said, "So are we okay, you and I?"

Her mouth was full. She brought her hand to cover her lips as she said, "Absolutely."

Chapter Five

2 P.M. Saturday, October 15, 1995

Walt and the team of two were down in the lower basement functioning as though they were a historical dig team. The area, cordoned off by heavy string, made into square areas for them to hunt. A deft hand cleaned dirt away with soft sweeps of a brooms bristles, unearthing evidence grain by grain. An echoing sound followed their every movement their every sigh. Two young men worked shoulder to shoulder, a sweat glowing over their foreheads. Hunched as always, Walt kept his back to the wall near the stairway. Partly to make sure no one else came into his crime scene, but mostly because he couldn't get down on his knees anymore.

The fellows found small pieces of metal, old screws without their heads and bits of wire. The blond sat back and worked on a lump of dirt. "Got something here, Lieutenant. It's a hinge I think, an old one by the looks of it." The soil came off bit by bit and revealed the full nature of the old rusty hinge.

Walt knit his eyebrows together thinking that they were uncovering a pile of discarded farm junk. At least that's all they seem to have discovered in what Walt initially thought was a grave.

The dark-haired officer stood up and walked over to Walt. He uncapped a bottle of water and drank as best he could from a leaning position. Walt asked him if he had found anything yet and the fellow shook his head. It was going to be a long afternoon. "Why don't we just dig up these graves?"

Walt reached in his pocket for some gum and pulled the pack out and offered Oliver one. The young man took the stick and unwrapped it as Walt answered. "I want all the evidence. Never know what might clinch the case."

Oliver sighed, capped his jug and lowered his body to his knees. Soon he'd brushed more dirt away from an area, making the earth smooth. "I'm not coming up with anything."

"Want a stick of gum?"

Dunham got up and took the gum from Walt, nodding a thank-you.

Pointing toward the sectioned area, "Keep at it," Walt said. He studied the dirt the guys were working and decided that they would work a little longer, and if nothing else showed up, a body perhaps, he'd have them take a shovel to it and find out what was under those three suspicious humps.

Police work often seemed dull, and Walt knew that from long hours at the job, but when it all came together, and it did with good detective work, you felt a high like no other. He unwrapped his gum and crumpled the paper and stuffed it in his pocket, all the while thinking about what he was going to tell Art.

He knew Art was gnashing his teeth to get down here, but he couldn't let him in on this part of the investigation. Art and Jim Wexford were too close, and he couldn't allow Art to give any information to Wexford. If that man was a part of this in any way, Walt was going to find out. A friend of Art's or not.

The afternoon drug on with bits and pieces forming a pile in the corner. Years of farm tools and equipment made Walt curious since this was underground and not near the surface where you'd expect to find discarded items like these. How and why are they here?

About five Walt called a halt and told the guys that they would be heading out for the day and tomorrow they would use shovels and open the mounds completely. They filed past him and climbed the dirt stairs, leaving Walt to ponder the area by himself. After a long moment he turned each helicon light out, letting the place darken and swallow its secrets once again. Walt followed his flashlight's beam upward, glad to get to the main basement floor. He walked over to the chains and ran the light over them, checking for any information they revealed. They were forged by a local blacksmith he surmised as they were handmade. Did these people have slaves in the area back in the nineteen hundred? Walt would need to check that out. The cuffs were rough in texture but strong.

Walt left them and walked back upstairs to the first level of the house. He'd not gone through the place yet. It was easy to see why Wexford would want to refurbish this old home. It had a grandeur and a flavor of the past. But lots of work to get this place back in shape, glad it's not my job to do. *Walt realized how happy he was in his one-bedroom apartment he had downtown. He wasn't home all that much anyway.*

He headed up the stairs. They wound gracefully up to the second-floor landing, and he walked from room to room. Wexford hadn't moved entirely into the home. He was working on it a little at a time. Walt found the place he was using for his bedroom. Spare of furniture. It all made sense to Walt. Wexford probably didn't know anything about what was in the basements. Basements? A house with two cellars. That's weird. Walt finished his tour and returned to the top of the stairs and surveyed the downstairs. These old houses had lots of walls and doors with heavy adornments. Another good reason to have his apartment. Way too much work to keep all this up.

Going down the stairs, he recorded every detail in his mind. The house had an eerie feel to it. Like a funeral. A quiet deaf sense. Walt shook it off and made it onto the first floor. He walked to the other rooms finding a library and what seemed like a sitting room. There was one large room, and it must have served as the hosting room for parties and such. He couldn't help himself. The sense of the times back there came to him, and he imagined the people and their attire. A massive fireplace filled with a roaring fire. A grand piano there and someone playing lively music. People laughing or singing along. Somehow the place took on life while he stood there soaking in the space.

As the reverie gave him joy, the next thought ripped that away. Something sinister went on here. It had become his job to find out what and when. Walt accepted the position without qualms. It indeed was different from most investigations. He doubted that he would be getting into anything new or relevant to today's crimes. And because of that, he didn't know how much time he'd be putting into this case. If it were already a closed case, he'd need to find that out. They'd come tomorrow and uncover those mounds, and tonight he'd get information on the old history concerning this place.

Walt locked the front door and saw that the all-night officer was here to take over until morning. No one would get in or out of this place, and no one would come onto the property without him learning who and why. He nodded to the officer and headed for his car.

Back at his desk, Art's old desk, he picked up the phone. "Art, Walt, can you come in now and have a little chat with me?"

"Sure, I'll be down in, oh say, twenty minutes."

Art hung up and put his coffee mug in the sink. He headed upstairs to freshen up, and a joy circled in his tummy. He was going to headquarters. He'd see everyone and get an update on this new case. Art splashed water on his face and straightened his mustache, running his hands through his hair to settle it in place. He grabbed a fresh shirt and managed to get it on and button it without his arm screaming at him. Things were getting better.

Art trotted down the stairs and called out to Melissa, "Honey, I'm going to the department."

"Okay."

He opened the front door, hit the garage door opener and scanned the neighborhood as he waited for the door to fully open. Art drove to the station and entered the detective area to "HI's" from a dozen people. It made him feel good right away. This was home to him, having spent so much time here over the last years as the lieutenant of homicide

Tracy greeted him with a hug, and he squeezed her arm, "Hey, girl, how are you?"

"I'm fine, how are you? Any word on coming back?"

Art shook his head, and they parted as he entered his old office and took the chair across from Walt, the chair Walt always sat in. He looked around, Walt had left the room the same. That was nice. "Hey."

"Hey, thanks for coming in. I didn't want to come to your house and talk about this case."

Art nodded understanding. "Find anything you can talk about?"

Walt bonded his eyes with Art's and shook his head. "We've found nothing but bits and pieces of metal, old stuff from farming by the looks of it."

"No bodies?"

"Maybe tomorrow. We will take the shovels in tomorrow and open the mounds up. Art, I need a title search of Wexford's property, and I have started Tracy on the back history and ownerships of the property from the newspaper's dead files. Once we know all the players some more refined history may show up. I'm looking for any opened cases over the years concerning that address. When I get all the information things might shape up. Right now, I don't have anything more than what you saw with your own eyes. The reason I called you in here is that from now on you are out. No more information from this office will be supplied. You are going to have to wait for the result, whatever and whenever that may be."

Art sat back in the chair, shocked at his old partner. He'd become the first Lieutenant. "I understand. Thanks for the heads up." He didn't understand, not one bit. What was Walt trying to do, cut him out of his job? Hell yes. That's just exactly what he's up to. Everyone else eligible for my position would be doing the same thing. Sharpening their resumés. Art rose and shook Walt's hand. He walked out of the office and down the hall past all the desks, nodding to each person as he stepped along. It felt funny and yet Art knew something had changed. Like something had ended, a door had slammed shut. He walked in a haze of wonder back to his car.

Chapter Six

2:54 P.M. Saturday, October 15, 1995

A rt walked out of the station, missed hearing the birds sing, the breeze pushing the tree leaves around, all the sounds he associated with his work and home and the peace in his life. He drove home fighting off anger and the sense that he should forgive Walt. After all, they had been friends, closer than friends, for so many years. Doesn't that count for anything? Apparently not! Walt had taken over and pushed him out, in effect letting Art know he would not be getting any information on the Wexford case.

On one level, he understood. Wexford was staying with him while the police went through his property for evidence in a crime scene. Walt didn't know what he had yet, so he was just covering his ass. Art got all that, but there was something more. The way Walt had treated him. There came a sever in their relationship as sharp as though a knife had sliced down between them.

Maybe if he gave Walt some time, and maybe if Walt found out that Jim wasn't involved, he'd come back around. And maybe, this one Art hated to think about, perhaps Walt likes my job. He's damn sure got a taste for it now.

No. That wouldn't be Walt. It must be the case that he wants to keep control of. It's what I would do. Art twisted his neck to allow the stress to ease off as he walked through the door and into the kitchen.

Jim sat at the table just putting his mug down as Art joined him. "Hey."

"Hey. Are you settling in okay?" Art went to the sink and drew a glass of water, he turned as he set the empty glass on the counter.

"Yes, thank you. Did you learn anything at the police station?"

Art didn't want to let on that he'd been blocked from now on, but there was no way he could keep it hidden for long. "They haven't found anything yet, but it's an ongoing investigation, and they are not going to be telling any of us what they are finding, or not finding. Not until they are finished."

"I don't have any idea when I can go back home."

"Nope. Not now." Art walked over to the carafe and poured a mug for himself.

"I don't know what I am going to be doing with myself, I have been working at the house, and you are my only client now. Hope you don't get sick of seeing my pretty face around here."

Art studied that face. When Jim smiled he squinted his eyes into crescents and Art wondered if he could see anything. His cheeks mounded smooth and pink while the lips stayed tight together. Art came to sit by Jim, scooting his chair out just as Melissa entered the house and called out.

His chin shot up and he said, "In here, honey."

Melissa strolled through the doorway and smiled at Art and at Jim. "I just finished babysitting for Nicole's kids. They are growing like weeds. Going out to Midnight now, any chance I can catch a ride?" Her words ran on with such youth and vigor.

Art grinned with pride. This was the first-time Jim met Melissa. "I can take you. How long do you think you are going to be?"

Melissa swung the refrigerator door open and took out the makings for a sandwich. She grabbed the pickle jar and a fork from the drawer to stab a big dill and place it on a plate. Melissa spread mayonnaise liberally and squirted some mustard and then peeled off some sliced turkey, putting that on top of some red onion slices. She put the other slice of bread on top and took a soda from the back of the refrigerator, all the while chatting about her day and barely taking a breath. She grabbed the sandwich up and chomped down … "be at the stables about three hours. Got to brush him down…"

"Mel, don't talk with your mouth full. Honey, this is Jim Wexford, a friend of mine. He's staying with us for a little while. His house is being worked on."

"Hi, glad to meet you." Melissa took his hand and shook it then returned to her sandwich. She snapped the cap on the soda and lifted the can to her lips.

"Nice to meet you too." He watched her put everything back in the refrigerator and when she went back to eating he said, "I'd just like some idea of how long it's going to be before I can get back to work out there. I feel useless and odd."

"Odd?"

"Yes. Out of place."

"Well, you have been displaced."

"I'm kinda sorry I told you about the basement."

Art smiled, "No you're not. You are curious about those lumps and those chains as much as I am."

"Yeah." Jim walked over and refilled his cup, passing Melissa as she was rinsing up from her sandwich.

She finished the soda and tossed the can in the basket. "I'm going to run Daisy outside, and then I'll be ready to go." She ran to the cage and got the pup out.

"That's a cute puppy."

She held Daisy to her cheek and cuddled her. "Thanks, my Mom gave her to me." Melissa and Daisy went outside and left Jim and Art looking at each other.

"She's lovely Art. And from what I see, she's well grounded. You can be proud of her and your job as a father."

Art grinned and sipped his coffee.

"So, what's going on over at my house?"

Art raised his eyebrows and began, "Well for starters they are going to find any evidence. That means they are going to leave no stone unturned, at the same time Walt is going to turn up the history of the house. Who owned it, when and where are they today? He's going to find out if there are any open or closed cases involving this house. The when and where of that information. Fact-finding is the mission he's on now."

"And, he's not going to let you help?"

"Not if he's any good at his job. He's not going to want you to know anything about what he's finding or found. He wants anything involving you to stay unspoiled."

"But I don't know anything."

"He doesn't know that, and until he does, you and I are on the back burner."

"This is not good for me, this is the kind of stuff that sends me to the bottle." He raised his mug, "Coffee just doesn't calm me."

"It's not supposed to, it's meant to get you going."

"My point exactly. Is there anything I can do to help the process along? We told him we'd come in and make a statement. Why don't we do that?"

"We will, just as soon as he asks us in. See, first Walt wants to know all about this case, then he'll ask you questions he knows the answers to just to get your response. If you come clean, all is good, if you don't, he's going to know it."

"That seems dishonest, tricky. I don't' have anything to come clean about. I don't know anything about that house except what I've unearthed while working on it. I can't be held for anything that happened before my time."

"No, you can't, and you won't. Walt's a good cop, he'll get to the bottom of all of this as soon as he can. Until he does why don't you make use of the pool, pretend you are on vacation. At club Franklin."

Jim got up and walked to the sink. He rinsed out his mug and set on the side next to the carafe. "I will need to buy some swim clothes, so I guess I should go shopping. That will keep me out of trouble this afternoon."

"Good idea, and could you look after Daisy? Let her out of the cage and out into the backyard a couple of times?"

"Not a problem, I like dogs."

"Okay, then. I will run Melissa out to the stable and be back here after I make an errand run. See you later."

Art headed for the garage and met Melissa there, they rode out to the stables, and Art found Charlie and paid the stable rent for the next six months. "Sorry I was late Charlie; my life is so messed up that I am letting things get in the way. I promise to do better by you in the future."

Charlie slid the cigar around in his mouth and managed a crooked smile as he placed his hand on the top of the pitchfork. He looked down at Art's hand and the money. "Mr. Franklin, no rush. I know you are going to take care of Midnight. I enjoy having Melissa and that horse here."

"Well, I just don't want you to think I'd stiff you."

"I'd never think that Mr. Franklin." Charlie took the money, shoved it in his back pocket and nodded to Art. He turned away, and Art turned his attention to Melissa. "Hey, are you okay with Jim being there at our house?"

She stopped wiping Midnight with a cloth and turned to her dad. "Who is he and why is he there?"

"Jim is my friend, and he bought a house, one of the old historical houses out at the edge of town. He found something suspicious in his basement, and the police are now considering it. That's all I know. He needed a place to stay, and I offered. He going to be with us a few days, at least until Walt tells him he can go back."

She nodded and picked up the brush and pulled it over Midnight's hips leaving the hide glistening.

"You take good care of Midnight, honey. It shows. Do you know how proud of you I am? I don't tell you that do I. Well, I am."

Melissa dropped the brush and came to her father, pushing against his chest and snuggling her head and placing her crown under his chin. "Oh, Dad, I love hearing that."

He could feel her shake and knew she wept. He let his arm tighten around her as they stood in the stable together. The smell of hay, the dust particles dancing on the shaft of light slicing from a crack in the wooden wall, and the mewing of the stable cat seemed to Art to comfort them as he stood there with her. He couldn't help but think where had his baby gone? Here stood a maturing person he loved with his whole heart. Boy, could he use a cigarette right now. It's a good thing that bet's still on. I don't smoke, and she doesn't get married until she's at least twenty-five. I wonder if she remembers making that bet? He squeezed harder but didn't ask.

"Dad, my driving classes. They start next month, and you have to have insurance and sign something."

"Okay, honey. I'll take care of it." That means another car in our family soon. I knew this day would come.

Chapter Seven

3:30 P.M. Monday, October 16,1995

"How are things going at your place?" Amanda slipped her hand into Art's as they strolled along School Street and the mustard colored sidewalk, past storefronts historically out of the fifties that once held J.C. Penney's, Woolworths and Karl's Shoes. Now they are filled with second-time around items looking for new homes, trendy eateries, and wine tasting venues.

Cars passing were mirrored in those windows as they looked in. Reaching the corner, they stepped down on the pavers at the intersection and Art squeezed Amanda's hand, totally enjoying School Street with her.

"Have you been here at the Farmers Market?"

Art nodded and glanced at his watch, it was three thirty as they strolled along. He spotted an open table out front of a pub and motioned to her, and she followed him to a chair. He scooted it out for her, and she sat. They weren't seated very long when the waiter arrived with menus. After choosing they relaxed back, breathing in the warmth of the afternoon and drifting away from their lives with the many complexities.

"Melissa's going to be driving soon. She starts driving school next month."

"Are you ready for that?"

"As ready as I will ever be."

The waiter brought drinks and a colorful platter of starters. They centered on that, fingering the food, tasting and savoring.

"Good."

"Art, tell me about your childhood?" Amanda picked a slice of cheese and placed it on a square cracker.

The breeze blew through the trees and rustled the olive colored leaves as he began. He first wrinkled his nose as he grinned. His mustache danced as his lips changed shape. Art's eyes twinkled impishly. "I was the center of attention in the Franklin family. They just couldn't get enough of me." A broad, toothy show to let her know he was joking.

She stopped eating and pointed her finger at him, "I bet you were." Her eyes sparkled.

They talked confidently now, and he could see she savored their connection.

"I want to know how you were raised, what expectation you might have for our child if we were to raise one of our own." A bright pink rushed over her cheeks, finding her temples before stopping.

He nodded, sipped his beer. He'd never, even with Evelyn, talked to another woman like he spoke with Amanda, "Well, let's see." Art's hand, involved now, flitted like a butterfly, "I grew up in Oregon. My folks had a home on the river. It was a three-bedroom, one bath, one story. A house in the woods. Perfect place for kids to grow up. We had a garage that was back from the house on a long driveway, and one falling down barn. I had chickens and a goat to take care of and a dog. A big black lab. I called him Barker. He loved the water as much as I did. He was my swimming buddy, and we were there every minute possible. I have a brother and a sister, Nick and Ruthie. You'd like them. Ruthie and her husband are into antique cars. My brother and sister are still in Oregon, and they have their own families now. I am the oldest, so their kids are a little younger than Melissa." Art sipped again. "I don't see them much. Not after my Mom and Dad passed. Never gave it any thought until now. Guess I've just been busy." Art ate some cheese and crackers.

"You didn't tell me what Nick does."

"Nick," Art smiled, "Nick is a businessman. You can't get him away unless it's to play bridge. He loves the game and is a master at it, so is Ruthie."

"Do you play?"

"I play at it. I haven't in a long time. I'd probably need lessons."

"Would you like to see them? We could drive up one weekend. While you are out of the homicide business, you could take a little time. Maybe they would like to come to our wedding." She looked deep into his eyes.

He sat back. "We could." Art's world was changing by leaps and bounds. Some of it scared him, like, was he ever going to be back to the homicide division of the Lodi Police Department? *What was going to happen with Melissa now that she's sixteen, and she wants to drive, and become a pilot? Does she still want to be in the police force?* Art grabbed his upper lip with his lower and pulled down on his mustache the gears twirling in his brain. Everything he thought would be in his future seemed to be fading fast. His eyes centered back on hers, the pools of blue that he loved so much. He recalled back to that afternoon at the Doc's by the rose garden, where he proposed to Amanda. He had held her hand, and they were talking about what had happened with Melissa's mother and how Melissa had told her that we were going to marry and become a family.

My proposal was undoubtedly flimsy. It embarrassed Art now that he thought about it. He'd merely said. 'Well, what do you think, how about marrying me and living happily ever after.' She'd said 'yes' and that was that. Not very romantic and women ate that stuff up, he knew that from all the conversations he'd overheard from Melissa and Sandy over the years.

Here we are today. Art looked around. The sun showed on the window of the shop across the street. Art decided the afternoon couldn't be more beautiful for what he wanted to do. A grin pulled his lips and allowed his teeth to peek through. He rolled over on his hip, reached into his pocket and, pulled out a sapphire-blue velvet ring box and set it on the table, opening the lid for her to see inside. The set glistened and sparkled. He saw her eyes jump when she understood.

"Honey, I called you and asked you to stroll down School Street with me because I thought that we haven't had a very good start. I wanted to change that." He got down on one knee. She drew her eyes from the set to his kneeling form.

"Amanda, it's fall. The leaves are changing color, soon they will drop, and life will appear dormant. But not really, there's a hidden rebirth building, and it will push forth for all the world to see. You're my life, my love…will you accept this ring and become my wife for all time and all ages? Will you join me in the new birth, a new beginning?"

She put her beer shakily down and brought her hands to both sides of his face, gently placing them lovingly. She considered Art's left eye and then the right and smiled as tears formed, glossing hers. "You make me so happy. You don't do anything wrong. And, yes. My love."

He picked up the box and slid the rings free and held the engagement ring up for her finger to slip through. She brought her finger up, and he placed the ring, feeling the warmth of her hand as he slid the diamond in place. "Do you like the it? I thought about letting you pick it out, and then I decided I wanted to do that and surprise you."

She held her hand out, and they looked at the ring. "This is one surprise I will cherish all my life."

Art's heart took flight, everything lately seemed right and peaceful. Peaceful is the one sense he savored, as last July peace had been ripped away from him, and he thought for a long time that he'd never feel calm again. She brings me harmony. He grinned at her as she gazed at her ring, the look on her face telling him everything he wanted and needed to know. He'd scored a bullseye. With all his might he withheld the desire to jerk his arm up and bringing it down making a "Yes!" sign.

After a long silence between them, they rested back in their seats and picked up their beers, toasted the glasses together and sipped.

"Now, my love. Continue. What sort of kid were you? Naughty or nice?" She asked.

A smirk told it all and Art licked his lip before going on with his tale. "I was not the nicest of children. I found myself into things that were not my business, and my mother sat me down many times to explain the facts of life to me. Since she had to do that many times, it seems I didn't listen too well."

"So, our kid might well be a little terror?"

44

Art tipped his head and nodded. "You probably were the perfect little lady, and that might offset my tendencies. But then, you are always telling me what a great job I've done with Melissa."

"That's true. Mel's a great kid. Not like you were at all." She became serious, "Me." She hummed. "One would only hope, but alas, that is not the case. I was a bit of a hard head myself."

"You? No, it's not possible."

She nodded, "Oh yes, it is possible. Were you ever arrested?"

Surprised Art jumped forward in his seat, "You were arrested?"

"No. Not really. Just almost."

Art's elbows noisily hit the table, he knit his fingers together and set his chin on them. "Okay, give. I want the whole story, so I know just what I am getting into."

Their bodies came together with her hands circling her beer as they talked.

She whispered, "I had a B-B gun and some of the other kids, my age kids, thought it was a real gun, and they called the police, and I had a long talk with a man in black. He almost took the gun, but when I convinced him that the gun the kids saw was this gun that I was showing him, he let me keep it. All us kids played cowboys and Indians when I was growing up."

Art gave a severe glance, "Come on, there's more to that story. What did you do that got that policeman out there?"

She continued. "Well, if you must know."

"I must."

"The nosy cop in you?"

"Probably."

M.L. WEATHERINGTON

"I don't really remember how it all started. I was about ten or eleven. We lived out of town about two miles. My folks had a house on a large lot. Almond trees grew on all sides but one, the one that faced the road. We had an old rinky-dink shed, and I used it as my play place. Can't really call it a playhouse, it wasn't a tree house and the only things I did out there were run around and hide and play cowboys and Indians with my friends. There was this old wire fence, kind of swaying down in places because of the posts that leaned in, it ran across the front of the property. It didn't really keep anything out, but it was my line, and you didn't cross it, if you know what I mean. Friends on one side, enemies on the other.

These kids teased me, and I didn't like it, and I warned them to stop. Eventually, I got my gun and pointed it at Max. He was the bully of the gang of kids. I knew. I couldn't let him get the best of me. And he was the most significant target," Amanda chuckled, "Cause he was fat. I and told them that if they didn't stop what they were doing, I'd shoot. Then I would find myself the next big target, and I'd let them have it. They must have believed me because they took off running. And they brought back the cop."

Art laughed, sipped his beer while appraisingly her and said, "My Annie Oakley takes no prisoners."

Chapter Eight

8:35 A.M. Tuesday, October 17th, 1995

The meadowlark trills welcoming the new day. It's one of those mornings you just love to be out in. It's not too cold and not too hot, the birds are happy, flowers are blooming, and the air carries their scent. Somewhere in the distance, a dog barks.

"Detective Culpepper?" Officer Oliver said as the shovel clanked against the side of the Ford as he lifted it from the back of the County pickup truck. "Do you want us to dig the mounts up or should we still be careful?"

Walt narrowed his eyes, felt his pocket and pulled a toothpick free from its confines and placed it in his mouth. It waggled as he spoke, "Be careful, at least until we unearth something that defines our search, but not like yesterday, we dig today."

The men turned and together observed the old house as though men condemned. They stood silent and the meadowlark trilled again. Resolutely, they walked into the house carrying the excavating equipment and worked their way down to the bottom basement. Cold met them as they put their things down and lit the lanterns and turned off their flashlights.

"It's like working from the inside of a grave. Creepy," Oliver's voice echoed.

Walt chewed on his toothpick and nodded in agreement. "And the sooner we finish, the better, better.... better." The men had grown used to the echoing of their words.

"I'll take that one." Nickelson said, moving to the farthest mound. The blade of his shovel bit into the ground, he put his foot on the edge and leveraged his weight pushing the blade deep down. Off came his foot and he lifted the dirt and turned it over in a new pile. Oliver's shovel sliced into the earth again and the two labored steadily, moving one pile to another. As they worked, they uncovered what proved to be more household refuge. Old light bulbs from an early era, rusted tin cans, broken glass. Nothing sinister. "I think you can date this house by this garbage," said Oliver.

"You can." Walt hung his head. This was the regular everyday hour upon hour drudgery of police work where you keep examining things that will never matter, watching for that one thing that does. "Keep working."

The two had perspiration blooming over their foreheads. Even though it seemed cold in the basement, it was close, and no abundant fresh air made its way down here.

"I need the light over here," Oliver said as he repositioned his lantern.

"Find something?" both Walt and Nickelson asked.

"No such luck."

A half hour passed, and both men were drenched. The mounds they were working were open, and nothing of police interest had been uncovered.

"This is a total waste of time," Nickelson said.

Walt looked from one officer to the next. "Get the last mound uncovered and if this is all we find we are done. There's no crime here."

Both men moaned as they turned to the last heap and moved over to start work. As the shovels chewed away, Walt called a halt. "Let's go up and get a cup of coffee. I think it's time for a break."

As they stepped out on the porch, an officer approached Walt and handed him a note. Tracy wanted him to call in. He smiled to the officer and made his way to his car. He sat down and picked up his phone. She answered on the first ring. "Whatcha got?"

"Wexford's owned this place just sixty-one days. He took possession August the third. The house was on the market for six years. It was off the market for a year and back on a year. It's been on and off the market. No buyers until the Doc. According to what I 've found on the Doc, he came from Arizona. Looks like he just happened to pick this place to buy, Walt. No connection at all. He got his license to practice psychiatry and applied to California and has been accepted to practice here."

Tracy stopped talking while shifting some papers around, "The place belonged to the Whitmore's. Abigail Nancy Whitmore was Gregory Whitmore's widow. He had a tailor shop in town. He was influential in running Lodi. And we're talking late 1880's. It stayed in the family through the years until the last family member died. Douglas Whitmore died—in 1978. The town condemned the house when they found his body in bed. Seems old Dougie was a hoarder."

"Be respectful Tracy!"

"Sorry Walt."

Walt chewed on the toothpick as he listened to Tracy. "Thanks, Tracy. I'll be in the office later."

"You're not finding anything?"

"Nope, garbage."

"Sounds about right for that place."

Walt hung up and turned to see the fellows huddled together drinking coffee from the back of the pickup truck that had carried their work equipment to the site. He'd have them finish the last pile, then he'd stop them. Officially the police investigation would end and they'd be out of there in the next couple of hours. It made him sad, as Walt wanted to get the answers and ending like this just made him feel like he'd failed. He hadn't but that didn't change how he felt. On the other hand, he was glad nothing sinister had happened to anyone here, or so it now seems. "Let's wind this up and get back down there." Walt walked over and poured himself a paper cup full of hot coffee. He lifted it to the others and tried to sip the steaming brew.

"We about done here?"

Walt nodded, "Looks that way. We'll finish up down there. Make your reports and close this out.

Oliver looked at Nickelson, "Good. I hate it down there."

Nickelson shook his head as he poured the little remaining coffee on the ground. His shoulders dropped as he turned toward the house, his eyes leaving the damp spot and raising to take in the three-story home that looked so innocent. There was no crime here according to all that he'd personally unearthed. *What a waste of time.*

Walt drank the top of his coffee and poured the rest out. The sooner they got back to work the sooner they'd be done. He didn't want to be down there any more than they did. "Okay."

Dejectedly the three worked their way back to the dig site. The lights were turned back on, the flashlights turned off, and the shovels bit the dust again. Walt flipped his flashlight back on and moved over to the pile of refuse.

It's been a long time since anyone put anything in these mounds. *By the looks of this garbage, we can date this stuff. Bet you anything that it was in the 40's. I could probably call this off right now. What would Art do? I know what Art would do. He'd dig this whole place up until it was evident there was nothing else but garbage down here.*

The guys took a cue from Walt and stopped working, putting their hands on the tops of the shovel handles and watching him. When he noticed the sound of digging had stopped he said, "Get back to work."

"Awe, Walt, there's nothing here."

"Yeah, yeah." Walt shifted his toothpick. "Okay, let's clean this place up and get out of here."

"What do you want to be cleaned up?"

"Just get our stuff out of here and back to the truck."

"Do you want us to put the piles back in place?"

"No." Walt started for the stairs. "Just get our gear and leave the rest alone." The officers brought everything to the basement floor and shut the door to the lower area for the last time. They carried everything outside and put it back in the pickup truck.

Walt wondered about those chains, but nothing pointed to anything being wrong other than their existence. He guessed he'd always be wondering about them.

Chapter Nine

11 A.M. Tuesday, October 17, 1995

"Walt called me a while ago Doc. You can go back home any time you want. They didn't find anything in the basement but garbage," Art said as he came into the kitchen. "He just called a minute ago. They've finished."

The Doc smiled as he looked up from his letter. The pages laid on the counter. "That's great news. I'll get out of your hair today."

"Oh, the Franklin place isn't good enough for you now?"

The two laughed that nervous laugh when thanks are in order, but you don't know how other than to say thanks.

"The mail's in, great." Art sat down and sorted his pile of bills until he came to one piece of mail. Pulling it more to the center he studied it. Picking it up, Art used it to tap on the counter a couple of times. Realizing the doc was watching gave him a funny feeling in his stomach. What should be done about this envelope, this correspondence from Evelyn? It was not an expected letter, and in a colored envelope at that. What could she want? Art tapped it again, and the doc cleared his throat.

"You going to knock that letter out of its cover? You know there's a better way to extract that?"

Art swung his eyes toward the Doc, tightened his lips and made a clicking sound as the lips opened. "It's from Melissa's mother."

"Oh!" The doc set his jaw, "Not good news?"

"She usually writes once a month to say the money for Melissa's been transferred to my account."

"Maybe she just wants to tell you something or ask you something. You two are co-parenting, now aren't you?"

Art did that mustache thing again with his bottom lip, thinking about what the doc was saying. Finally nodding, Art slid his thumb behind the flap. "She's my child. I have full custody. Evelyn has her foot in the door, but that's all." He pulled along tearing the paper until it only needed him to tug the message free. Using his thumb and forefinger, the letter slipped out, and it lay exposed. 'Dear Art.'

That wasn't too scary.

'The reason for my communication is a phone call from Melissa. Telling me you and 'that woman' are back together. She said that you are planning to marry. I notice no time for that joining has been set. Is that because you have such a difficult time committing to another person? One can only wonder. Anyway, if you intend to marry her, then I must call our agreement complete and request you sell the house immediately and give me my share."

I await your response. Sincerely your Evie.'

Art tore up from the bar stool, striding toward the back door, spinning around and storming back to the letter. His hand smashed down on it and immediately gripped the whole of it, crumbling it into a ball which soon sailed into the kitchen sink.

The Doc followed him with wide eyes. "News not to your liking?"

Arts eyes were on fire and smoldered as he leveled them on the docs. "Evelyn wants me to sell the house now and give her half because I am engaged to Amanda. Seems Melissa told her about us."

"Oops! The soup thickens. What are you going to do?"

"What am I going to do? What am I going to do?"

The Doc watched Art make a circle of the kitchen. "Yeah, what are you going to do?"

Pacing past the doc, he said, "I could wring her neck."

"You'd go to jail."

Clinching his fists by his sides, he said, "It'd be worth it."

"Call her and work this out. You've got plenty of charm, my man. Use it."

Art's eyes smoldered. "I don't feel charming. I feel pissed."

"That's clear enough. Being pissed isn't making anything happen. It's just keeping you in place. You know better. And, right now who has the power?"

Art had to look at the doc. "Yeah, I know." As he calmed, he studied his feet. "Evelyn has sent money each month, so I could keep Melissa in one place while she grew up. We never even discussed what would happen if I found someone else. It wasn't even relevant at the time."

"Now it is?"

"Yes, I don't want to move Melissa. She needs to finish school and stay with her friends and what she is used to. At least until she's out of school and on her own. I always thought she'd have a home to come back to if something happened." Art's shoulders sank a bit as his voice lowered. "I don't know if a new place will feel like a home she can come running back to if she needs too."

"Well, call Evelyn and talk to her. Tell her Melissa needs this place... for how long?"

"She's sixteen now. Until she's eighteen? I don't know. I never thought of it. I don't want her feeling that I want her to move out because I am going to marry Amanda." The room silenced as Art thought. *Shit!* "This is turning into a mess."

"What's a mess?"

Art spun when he heard Melissa's voice. "Oh, nothing honey, just talking with the doc here. He's leaving us to go back home."

Melissa got a soda and snapped the can open and came to sit at the counter with Art and the Doc. She sipped and looked from one to the next. "I am going to babysit tonight. Got a new job."

Art turned to her, "Oh. Where?"

"The nurse that lives by Nicole's. I got her name and number and called her today. She works graveyard this next month and wants me to stay all night. I said yes." Melissa sipped again.

Art shook his head, "All night. What's this nurse's name?"

"Sheryl Clay."

"I don't think I like you staying all night."

"Her husband just died, in his sleep. She must work."

"There's no family she can count on?"

"I don't know. Nicole knows her. Why don't you ask her?"

"I will."

"Okay." Melissa sipped and looked from one face to the next. "What mess?"

Art cleared his throat, "Nothing."

The Doc chimed in, "My place.   It's probably a mess."

Melissa nodded changing her focus from one face to the next. She nodded again. It was all they were going to say on the subject. Didn't fool her one bit. Her Dad always had secrets, he'd had them all her life. Melissa slipped her hand into her pocket and brought out a paper. She opened it out and slid it across the counter toward her dad. "You've got to sign this to let me get a place in driving school. It starts next week."

The Doc stood, "Well since I can go back home I'd like to get there before dark today to see what's what. Are you interested in a walkthrough?"

Art read through the request pulled his pen and signed the form. Sliding it back toward her he said, "Do all things safely." He stared at her until she nodded.

Turning to the doc, he said, "I am."

"I'll get my things, and you can follow me over there."

Art walked over to the sink and picked up the crumpled wad from Evelyn and lifted the envelope. He looked at Melissa, wondering if he should tell her about the demand. A smile spread across his lips as he thought about how she was happy that he's found Amanda and they were going to be a family. Where are we going to be a family? God, if I must move now. He looked down at his arm. The weeks were adding up, and it didn't seem to him his arm was getting better. *I need to get back to work before the department gives my job away. If I should sell this house, there's so much that's got to be done. I could ask Jim to help me. He's got a pot full of work at his place.* The crumpled letter in his hand caught his attention. He'd call Evelyn as soon as he got back from seeing the Doc's place and what the police found or left. There are those chains, and I wonder what Walt figured out about them?

"Dad?"

"Yeah?" He turned to her.

"What's wrong?"

Art jerked his head. What was he saying with his body that would elicit that question from her? "Nothing Honey, I'm just having a bad day. My arm is not healing like I'd like it, and everything is getting to me. I'm sorry."

"You could tell me. I'm old enough now."

He smiled. "Yes, you are." He looked down, "You are so very special to me. And I want you to know how proud I am to be your dad."

A sparkle flashed in her eye as her cheeks reddened. She folded up the paper and put it back in her pocket.

"See ya. I'm going over to Jim's." Art left her in the kitchen as he checked on the doc and to ready himself to go over to the old house.

Walt was there on the front porch as the Doc and Art arrived. Walt handed Doc Wexford the house keys and said, "Let's sit a few minutes, and I'll tell you what I've discovered."

The men moved over to the seats on the porch. "We spent a couple of days down there and found garbage. Mostly household. It seems the lower basement was once the stable area of this house. According to the records, the house was added onto as the family's wealth dictated. In the early days, the stable was right behind the original house. All of it was located on river level ground. There's plenty of evidence that a tremendous amount of dirt was backfilled in this area. We found lots of horseshoes, hinges, and nails. Antique nails. If we could date the stuff we turned up, the last was in the thirties maybe. Nothing sinister."

"Then I can go ahead and finish this house."

"As far as we are concerned nothing of interest was found here. It's all yours."

The doc sat back. "I'm relieved. Now I have to find a new handyman."

Walt bid them goodbye and left them sitting on the porch.

"So, it's back to tearing this place apart?"

"Yep. It's the only way to fix it right. Got to get down to the studs and start from scratch."

"Wow, I don't think I could tackle a job this big. I admire you."

"You probably don't know the difference between a left-handed hammer and a right."

Art looked at him a long moment. "I didn't know there was any difference."

"Just my sick way to lighten things up."

Chapter Ten

11:30 A.M. Tuesday, October 17, 1995

"Well, shall we go in and see what damage the police did or didn't do?"

The two walked into the house. Nothing seemed changed just dustier. They nodded to each other and headed straight for the basement. The doc's flashlight directed the way and showed the dirt had been moved from the three neat masses into humps with the waste product stacked in several piles, some glass, some metal. "Mostly rusted cast offs."

"Yeah, I'm going to clear it all out."

"You going to keep this space down here?"

"No, I'll just close it off. It's too tight down here."

"It would have been nice if they had found something of value."

"Not my luck."

"I think you were lucky. At least there's not an ongoing crime scene. That would tie the property up for months."

"True."

They moved back into the house and walked up the stairs to the second landing. "Let's look at the upper rooms." The doc led the way, and they climbed the final staircase, opening the door at the top of the landing. It had a circular shape to the area, and Art knew that he was standing in the turret room he'd seen from the sidewalk. He walked to the window and looked down at the street below. He saw the driveway and their cars, "Imagine what this place must have been like when there was nothing but fields around and acres of it. I think it must have been incredible up here back then. A much slower lifestyle." He noticed the window sill, a wide piece of pine that had once been painted a white or crème color. It had been touched by someone much smaller than he or Jim, leaving a clear set of prints the whole length of the fingers in the heavy dust. Art figured it probably was done by one of the female cops when they were going over this place.

They turned their attention to the room itself. "Someone really liked wallpaper."

"Someone loved roses." The Doc reached over and ripped the corner of the paper away exposing another layer of wallpaper. "I have a hunch this house stands today because of this crap."

They laughed.

Art shuffled to a stop, he leaned down, "Doc?"

"Yeah?"

"Did Stumper come up here?"

"No, why?"

Art pointed and picked up a butt. "Isn't that the kind of cigarettes he smoked?"

"Huh."

"That's new."

"One of the cops might have come up here."

I'll have a talk with Walt about this. "Yeah, that's probably true."

They moved over to a set of drawers sitting next to the entry door. An old flaking chest. The top drawer pulled out oddly as the doc coaxed it to open fully. It was empty except for a pack of cigarettes, the same kind as the butt Art had picked up moments ago. Both their eyes narrowed, and they looked at each other. "Stumper? No. Someone's been up here lately."

"You've got a squatter."

"I had no idea. I wonder when that started. Was he, or she, coming before or during the cops being here?"

"Good question. You're going to have to set a trap for this person."

"Could be a homeless person. Someone trying to get off the streets at night. This house was empty for a long time."

"That's probably it."

"Shit, if it isn't one thing it's another."

"I know. Let's see what's in the other drawers."

The doc pulled each open and found them empty. In the bottom drawer lay a packaged item the size of a child's football, and about that shape. "What's that?"

Art reached for it, "I don't know." He felt it and wrapped his hand around the bundle and brought it to the top of the dresser. "It's hard."

"Hard?"

"Yeah, stiff." Art looked at the doc, "It's yours, shall I open it here?"

The doc nodded, and Art pulled the loose end, carefully undoing the item. Both took their breath when the last of the paper peeled away.

The feet were drawn up, the claws long and sharp. The grey feathers a soft contrast against the crimson tail feathers.

"What's a dead parrot doing here?"

"Your guess is as good as mine." Art stooped and considered the drawer and pulled out some other items. A used-up roll of masking tape, a wooden ruler. Probably eighty years old if a day. Art turned it over in his hand. He'd used plastic rulers all his life, and this was a first for him. Over in the corner of the drawer was a clear container for holding a tape. The kind used for small recorders. He could see the tape was used and rolled halfway through. He knew he would play that tape and find out what was on it. Won't be anything, he told himself as he put the container on the top of the dresser by the carcass. "You wouldn't have a recorder that would play it?"

The Doc picked up the tape and shook his head. "No." After studying it, he set the tape on the countertop and turned from the dresser.

"I could get one from the department." After a moment Art said, "On second thought, I'd like to keep this to ourselves."

"No point bringing the cops back, especially if there's nothing on that tape."

"Exactly! That birds not been dead all that long. It's just beginning to stink. It also means someone's been up here recently."

"How do you figure that?"

"You didn't bring this bird and leave it in the drawer, did you?"

"No!" The Doc shook his head. "I've been on forced vacation. I want to get it out of the house. It's a good thing we came up here, see the trail of ants?"

"They would have taken care of the carcass."

"I'm going to have to set ant traps out."

Art looked around the empty room. "It's possible someone's been sleeping up here. Maybe they brought the bird and the cigarettes. The recording and the rest of the stuff from that drawer could have been there for some time. Well, maybe not the tape." He covered it with his hand and scooped it up, holding it with two fingers for the doc to see. "I think I'd like to hear what 's on this tape. I don't know. Just nosey."

"Take it, and that bird."

Art slipped the tape into his pants pocket. "You can have the bird."

"I'll bury it out back." The Doc gently picked up the bird by sliding his hand under the paper and setting it back around the body. "These are highly desirable birds and expensive. You know they can talk. Copy pretty carefully what they hear."

"Someone might be missing their bird. We can check the newspaper to see if anyone's placed an ad."

They moved out of the room, the Doc checked to see if he could lock the door and he could not, and they went back downstairs. The doc led the way through the kitchen and out the back door. He set the bird down on the sawhorse near his work area. "I'll have to get a shovel from the workroom. Can't help but wonder why the bird wasn't buried when it died?"

"I'm curious about that too." Art waved at him, "I'll get going and talk to you tomorrow. You have a good night, and well, I guess that's it for now."

Chapter Eleven

1:20P.M. Tuesday, October 17, 1995

The door squeaked as Art pushed it open, "Hey!"
From a distance came a wise crack answer, "Hey right back at cha."

Holding the small black plastic recording up for view Art walked into Tango Investigations like he owned the place. A smile plastered on his face as he came to a stop before Yvonne's desk space.

Her steely eyes covered by heavy eyebrows accentuated an unruffled, stony expression just before her lips moved, "And, you are here to apologize?"

Art brought his eyebrows together wrinkling his brow. "Apologize? For what?"

She nodded and rolled her jaw. "Are you that dense?" Yvonne pushed back in her office chair and leaned forward to stand.

He put his hand out to stop her. "No need to get up…"

"You're here to borrow something."

"Yeah." He cocked his head to the side. "How'd you know?"

"Because you only come here to amuse and abuse me. You're one of those people that look out for themselves and themselves only. You manipulate others for your own aggrandizement."

"Wow! That's a pretty big word for a… I don't abuse you!" Art took the orange personnel chair and sat, allowing his hand to come down and take the tape from view.

"And you don't do anything I tell you to do either."

His eyes sailed toward the floor as he thought, "You're talking about the last time I hired you?"

Yvonne's lips pouted, and lines formed like a frame around her lips, "Damn straight."

"You got well paid for all you had to do. So, what are you pissed about?"

"I'm," Yvonne got up, snatched her cane and steadied herself to turn from the desk. She took two steps, "pissed, as you put it, because, when I assume a case I intend to do my best to resolve the issue in my client's favor. I don't need two fronts to fight at a time. You are a loose cannon, my friend, her finger pointed. And I don't trust you. If you are here to hire my staff and me again, I 'm going to have to think long and hard before I take you back on, and you are going to sign a contract with me to stay at least one hundred feet away from any identified areas of interest."

"You know I was there in the field?"

She looked shocked, "What field?"

Shit! She didn't know. Now the cat's out of the bag. She won't let this go until I tell her. Art brought his hand up, "I just wanted to know if you have a player for this tape. I'd like to hear what's on it."

He watched the wheels in her brain spin. Her eyes left him and glanced at the tape. "That's all you want?"

He bobbed his head.

"The cost will be the truth."

Here it comes. *Why don't I keep my mouth shut?* "What truth?"

"Are we going there again?"

"Guess so, you keep talking cryptically."

"The field, give." Those eyes were two, cold, calculating marbles shining back at him.

He nodded, there was no place to run. "I bought a camouflage suit and sat in the field under a tree the day you and Lessie checked out the backyard of my neighbors' house."

For a long time, those dark orbs stared. And if you weren't watching closely, you would miss the twitch at the corners of her mouth. She found this hilarious. She screwed up her lips, narrowed her eyes and reached into her desk. "This will play that. I don't want to hear it. So, you can take yourself in the inner office and listen to your heart's content."

He took the player from her and entered the inner room. The board with all the pictures was still up from his case, and he looked at all the faces again. There was a small desk off to the side set next to an electrical outlet, so he moved over there and plugged the unit in. He opened the plastic case and took out the tape. Sliding it in place, he pressed play. At first, he heard garbled sounds, nothing definite. After a long grainy silence, a bird screeched, and then a bird screeched again. Art rewound

66

the tape and turned up the volume. The same garbled sounds came before the screech. Could it be the same bird as the one found in the drawer? Why couldn't it? After all the tape was with the bird in the same drawer. He listened to more garble and then clear as a bell toll someone saying, "Don't shoot, Sway, don't shoot me!" The voice was off in the distance and not close by the phone and Art now realized that this tape came from a phone recorder. What phone recorder? He was about to turn it off when the bird made another sound and spoke openly in a deep male voice, "Sway, don't shoot me, Sway, don't kill me!" The bird changed its voice to that of a female, "Rio, you deserve to die. Bam, bam!" The bird made the sound of gunfire accurately.

It reminded Art of a play, not real people talking real talk. If someone was mad at another enough to shoot them would they sound like that? Probably not. Art made the judgment call that this was not a real murder case. He pressed his lips and pushed the off button. Art removed the tape and put it in his pocket. Walking back out to her desk he handed the machine to her and thanked her for its use.

"Nothing on the tape?"

"Thought you didn't want to know."

"I don't, but the look on your face says you didn't find anything cop exciting." She grinned from ear to ear.

"You're having fun at my expense."

Yvonne made that stony face again, but a sparkle in her eyes flashed just as a grin came slow and precise, "Every chance I get."

Art returned the smile and nodded, "So very glad to give milady amusement."

"Get out of here, and never darken my door again."

Art took two steps back, smiling, "You don't mean that."

"Don't I?"

"You'd miss me." Art closed the door behind him and walked through the parking lot to his car. He drove to the department and went in to see Walt. Everyone greeted him, and he took time with each one, telling them, he was mending as fast as he could and hoped to be back at his desk soon. Finally making it to Tracy's desk, he hugged her and asked to see Walt. She nodded and pointed to his old office door. "You know the way."

"Walt!"

"Art. Come. Sit."

He moved to the personnel chair across from Walt and tried his best not to look around the room to see if Walt had made any changes. It seemed Walt felt at home now in the office and that got under Art's skin a bit. "I just wanted to tell you that it looks like one of your guys went up into the tower room at the Doc's house and smoked a cigarette. He left a butt on the floor."

Walt shook his head. "No one of my guys went up there."

Oh, now it's his guys.

Art kept his face straight, "How do we account for the fresh butt?"

Walt shook his head, "None of my guys went up there."

"You're sure?"

"Yes. I'm the only one that went up there. I don't smoke, you know that."

Then there's someone else. Art felt for the tape in his pocket and said, "We found a dead bird in the bottom drawer of the old chest in that upper room and a package of cigarettes. And this tape."

Walt set his eyes on the plastic Art was holding. "What's on the tape?"

Art said, lets' play it and see what you think. Walt got the player out and set it on the desktop. He plugged it in and reached for the tape. Art gave it to him and he inserted it into the device and pressed play. When it was done Walt sat back and looked at the machine. "We don't have anything on the books that fit that profile. No bodies have shown up with bullets in them. No one ID'd as Sway. We could check missing persons, but I think that's just bull."

"Yeah, that's what I thought too." Art took the tape from Walt's hand. "Just wanted to make sure there wasn't anything to this."

Walt nodded.

Chapter Twelve

3 P.M. Wednesday, October 18, 1995

Satisfied that Walt had no interest in the tape Art walked out of the station, and to his car. The audio tape rested at the bottom of his pocket, and would until he took it out, and placed it on his side table by his bed.

In the morning Art, showered, dressed and went about his duties heading to the therapist for his arm exercises and evaluation.

These days ran smoothly, and he felt Amanda played a big part in that. A smile came easy at the thought of her. They would have lunch today, he glanced at his watch, that would be in two hours and a half. She planned a picnic for them and told him she would pick him up. A mystery, Art loved it on the one hand and hated it on another. Art didn't like mysteries he didn't know the answers to. The little boy in him wanted to beg the location from her, but he waited. She brought so many facets to his life now, so many different interests that he never in a thousand years would have thought of on his own.

Art pulled up to his house and parked his car in the garage. He left the car and walked to the garage door control on the wall by the door. That's when he heard her voice.

"Stop right where you are fella."

He stiffened, turned his neck to see her in a soft dress of creamy yellow. He admired how well it went with her hair. The neck was open in a V shape, and she had a single diamond flashing from a spot just down from her chin. The only other thing he noticed about her now was the dimples deepening as she smiled that welcoming smile she has just for him. It lit up his world.

"You are under arrest! Come with me, and I will read you your rights."

He turned wholly unable to hide his pleasure, he wanted to run to her, gather her up in his arms right there under his garage door for all the world to see. His heart soared his mustache twitched. "You are, are you?" He moved toward her smiling broadly, "Under what authority?"

Her chin shot up, her blue eyes flashed. "The authority of the United States of Bliss, by the jurisdiction of Cupid, and the power invested in lovers."

Art didn't miss the implication of her message. He went willingly, happily, peacefully, knowing why his heart raced. A state of grace he didn't want to ever lose plus as he reached her his lips found the softness of hers and he tasted. A moment later he took a breath and said, "And where are you taking me?" His finger clicked the garage door control on his keychain as he looked at her.

The grind began, and the door descended clunking to a stop.

She kissed him once more and reached for his hand. "Put this on." Amanda held a bright orange cloth out to him. Before he could protest, she stood on tiptoes and snugged it over his head pulling it down so that it looked like a bandana tied sloppily around his forehead. "Well, your head is bigger than I thought." Her hand rubbed the side of his face as she allowed herself to drop back down. "Fix it, Art."

The warmth of her hand lingered. *God, she smells so good.* "How?"

"So, you can't see."

"Don't think I want to do that."

"Art!" She pinched his arm. "This is my mystery date, you have to do what I say."

He grumbled, "Okay. After I get into the car. I don't need to get this arm hurt on the way."

"I wouldn't let you get hurt."

"Just the same, I'll do it after we get into the car."

She took him by the elbow and guided him to the rider's side of the car, she opened the door and held his head so it would not hit the car as he sat down. When he sat safely she told him to put on the blindfold, then when she felt satisfied he couldn't see she made sure his seat belt was secure. "We're off."

Art managed to leave the material high on his nose, and he could see a little of his knees. He'd have to raise his head to see anything of value, but he felt happy for this little control. He'd let this be his little secret. His grin widened. "Don't you need to get in first?"

"Funny man." Amanda shut the door. He listened to her coming around to the driver's side. She got in and started the car. Art began to silently count. They rode through traffic until he heard gravel crunching and Art knew they were in the country. He practiced remembering things about this drive so that he could recollect later. Practice for the cop in him. The car slowed and turned, rolling down a long stretch to a stop.

"We are here."

She helped him out of the car, and he said, "Okay that I take this off now?"

"Yes."

He pulled it down and experiences a sense of peace, clear skies wide with fleecy clouds and a green field-stretching wide and far can bring. He dropped his head and saw the roses blooming so late in the fall. A sweet scent drifted to him. She led him toward a large boulder at the brink of a pond crowded with bushes and trees of different colors that cascaded into the water and mirrored back. "Where are we?"

"A friend of mine owns this farm. I asked to use the place for a little while this afternoon. Come on, we can see the Koi better over here."

Art stepped to a wooden wharf. Two blue Adirondack chairs waited, and he took the picnic basket from her and placed it by one of the chairs. He strolled over close to the edge, and the fish swam close working their mouths. Amanda sank down and pet the back of one of the white fish with an orange spot on its head.

"Tell me you haven't named that fish."

She laughed, "No. But, Art, aren't they pretty?"

"Absolutely. I didn't know fish were so friendly."

"They have learned how to get food." She turned the top of the rock to the left, and it opened to a container of food. She sprinkled a handful of fish pellets over the water, and it boiled with thrashing fish.

"Gosh, look at them go."

Amanda got to her knees, and he helped her to stand. They moved to the chairs and sat down.

He took in a deep breath and looked around seeing the car parked on the grass and beyond an orchard of walnut trees. He turned back to her, "This is really beautiful. I thought I knew all the properties in the Lodi area, but I don't know this one at all. You surprise me every day. Look at those two ducks. They are Mutt and Jeff. I think one is the boy and the other the girl. Look how gentle they are, beaks together like that. They don't have a care in the world. We should live like that. Whose property is this?"

"My friend's name is Jan Slamery. She's a retired nurse and lives in the big house, you will see it when we go back out." She opened the basket and pulled out some wrapped sandwiches. "We're in Galt."

Art's eyes widened, he didn't realize he'd gotten that far out of Lodi. "How much time do you have?"

"I have a four o'clock, so," she looked at her watch, "two hours."

Art reached for a sandwich and pulled out a bottle of beer. He took the chilled bottle and held it for her to remove the lid. He sighed. "This is nice." He clinked bottles with her. "Have you noticed how often you and I are eating nowadays. Every time we get together, it's a picnic or something centered around food."

She nodded.

He took a bite of his sandwich. Chewed, caught her eye, swallowed and said, "I got a letter from Evelyn. It's a sore subject with you I know, but" ... He studied her expression and saw she was receptive. "I thought you should know what she's up to now."

The sandwich, inches from her lips, waited, "Tell me?"

"She's demanding that I sell the house and give her half the proceeds. I don't want to do that right now. I would like for Melissa to finish out her schooling with the same surroundings. I always thought she would be coming home to the house she was raised in. Geeze, I don't know." He took a swig of the beer and looked out over the pond.

"Honey, that's something I wanted to talk to you about. We plan to marry, right?" She touched her ring and moved it around on her finger centering the diamond, admiring it while waiting for him to respond.

"Yes."

"Well," she nibbled the tip of her sandwich and chewed until she could swallow. "I don't want to live in a house with a history that never included me."

Shocked. Art believed she liked sitting with him in the backyard. The sandwich hit the bottom of his stomach and felt like a stone. His world spun out of his control yet again. "I didn't know you felt that way."

"We need to make our own home with our memories."

Things were moving too fast for Art.

"And, Art we need to set a date."

"For what?" Art looked at her.

She raised her eyebrows and waited for him to catch up.

At last, he grinned, "Oh. That date." He took a swig. "What were you thinking?"

She smiled, "I thought, wouldn't it be something to get married at Jim's house and gardens."

Art's expression said loud and definite, are you crazy. "The house is a mess."

"It won't be, and we could help Jim finish it. I could paint, and you could help him too. He'd let us I am sure. What do you think?"

"It's a long time, he's probably a year out. Is that too long for you?"

"Well, you have some loose ends to tie up and so do I, a year sounds about right. How about we ask Jim and if he says yes, let's get married one year from today. Melissa will be seventeen, she'll be in her last year at high school. Is she planning to go to college?"

"Yes." He scanned the ground by his feet, "She's going into the police force so she will be getting her Criminal Justice Bachelor's degree out of the way first. She wants to understand the court's system and then she'll have the Academy to go through, that's nearly five years down the road from now. I need to help her until she's ready to stand on her own."

"Of course, she would stay with us."

Art nodded. In his mind, a question circled around, and acid churned in his stomach turning the sandwich into a burpable.

"I am glad we figured this out." She ate with relish, sending the sandwich down with the beer.

Art held his lunch with three bites taken out, not at all sure he could finish it now. He lifted the bottle and drank. What was happening? How did it happen that females were giving him his walking orders? Gas built up, and he puffed his cheeks and swallowed it down.

"How's your arm?"

Art looked down at it, "I don't think it's any better and the therapist said today that she was sending a report to my Doctor. Not sure what that means other than I think she thinks I should be able to move my arm more than I can."

"You can't return to the department if your arm isn't better?"

"I can't pass fitness."

"There must be something you can do."

"I can't shoot with my left hand."

"Do you have to?"

Art nodded, "I need to be able to protect myself and others if need be."

She studied his arm, licked her lips and smiled as she readied the last bite of her sandwich to pop into her mouth. She looked up into his hazel eyes, "It will all work out."

The uneaten sandwich drooped in his hand so did his heart. He wasn't so sure.

Chapter Thirteen

3:30 P.M. Wednesday, October 18, 1995

Art stepped out of Amanda's car at the house and waved goodbye to her as he walked back to his front door, a smile plastered on his face. He didn't want her to know the panic that built with each new breath. Her car left the curb, and he slipped the key in the lock and opened the door. Peace and quiet surrounded Art as he stepped over the threshold and he leaned back against the closed front door and shut his eyes. He stood for a long moment to relish the sense of safety. At long last, he went upstairs and sat on the edge of his bed. His head hung, and his hand came up to cradle his forehead. The weak arm shook, and his heart pounded in his chest. He wasn't the man he used to be. Raymond McNamare took that from him, and there was nothing he could do about it now. He was losing everything. His job, himself, his home.

He had to call Evelyn and face this with her. God, he didn't want to, she's such a steamroller. He drove his right hand through his hair just as the next thought urged him to stand up. And, Amanda does not want to live here. Why can't things be easy? He paced the floor until he saw the red light on the answering machine and he wondered what that was all about. Could that be Evelyn? Staring at the red glow, he finally pressed the button and listened to the message.

"Art Franklin, this is the Medical Center. Doctor Spranger has your results back and wants you to schedule an appointment. Please call the office to make the appointment." Art sat on the bed and raised his finger, pressing to reset the machine.

"Dad?"

He looked up at his closed door, rose and walked the ten steps to open it and call to her. "Up here."

She bounced up the stairs and arrived at his door. "I am going to the stable to ride Midnight. I've got an all-nighter with the Nurse's kids. You okay?"

"Yeah, sure, why?"

"You don't look so good."

"Thanks." He brightened up and reached out to give her a hug, but she had backed away heading for her room. He watched her go, wondering how she would feel knowing that the house might have to be sold. He set his jaw.

Art headed for the kitchen and a cup of coffee. None had been made. He'd been up and out to the therapy on his arm at eight. He almost turned away to get a beer but thought better of it. The mood he was in might not be the best time to crack open a bottle.

Evelyn's letter waited crumpled in the wastebasket. He reached into his pocket and pulled out his personal list. Fingering down to her name he turned to the phone. *Answer on the first ring Evelyn.* The phone rang and rang, it didn't go to message. He finally hung up. *She's so frustrating.*

He heard Melissa running down the stairs. She would be in the kitchen soon. He brightened, making sure she found a more upbeat dad this time.

"Okay, I'm off. See you tomorrow morning." She carried her bag and went out the back door.

"Hey, are you taking that out to the stables?"

"No, going to drop it at Sharyl's house and then go to the stables."

She pulled her bike away from the stand as he got to the back door.

"Dad, Sharyl said she would go over some things on her car, so I wouldn't be so nervous."

Art nodded that he understood, but he didn't think he did. Just one more thing on his mind. He looked at her pushing the bike along the side yard to the front, "You be careful. That looks like a load."

"Soon I will be driving, and I won't have this problem."

He listened to the side gate close and went back into the house. "Egads! I've got to think about a car for her, and insurance." He spoke aloud to the kitchen walls. In kindness, they remained silent. *That term, I haven't thought about in years, my grandmother used to say it all the time. Egads. It's a great word. I like it.*

Art looked up Evelyn's number again and called her. She answered this time, and he was ready for her. "Hi, Evelyn." He paused, cleared his throat and looked around the empty kitchen. The walls needed painting, and he guessed the whole kitchen could use an uplift. "I have your letter." He ran his hand over the countertop,

"How dare you demand that I sell this house and give you your half now. Melissa is not out of school yet, she has the rest of this year and next. I don't intend to uproot her just to soothe your ego."

The line went still for a moment. "Well, I can talk with my attorney and see what he says. I'll get back to you later."

She hung up as Art said, "You do that, witch!" He brought the earpiece from his head and looked at it. If she was here, he'd have his hands around her neck and... Slowly he replaced the phone on the cradle. No, he wouldn't. He'd swore to serve and protect. He wiped his lips with his hand. *Don't let her get to you! She has no power unless you give it to her.*

The refrigerator door opened, and he grabbed a bottle of beer and walked outside. The kennel had been put up, and Daisy jumped up on the wire as soon as she saw him. He tipped his bottle toward her and said, "Okay, little girl you can come out for a while." He undid the latch and Daisy romped over the lawn and back to him, jumping against his leg. He smiled down at her and walked toward the boat dock. Daisy grew like a weed, not that she would be a big dog, but undoubtedly more substantial than when she arrived. Things were changing so fast, too fast. He hated the helpless numbness he'd been feeling. *If I can't go back to work what do I do for income?*

A swig of beer slid down his throat as the idea formed. Amanda would be supporting him. His stomach turned. *That would never happen. I could be a P.I. Could open my own business. Or...I could work for Yvonne. No, that probably wouldn't work. Why the heck not! There's probably plenty of things I could do for her firm. My arm would not be a factor. I know just about everything I need to know. One of the prerequisites is police procedural knowledge.*

Daisy worked her way to the water's edge, sniffing something of interest. Art watched, smiling at her playfulness. She saw enjoyment in every leaf, rock or blade of grass. She just loved for the sake of it. Oh, how he'd like to explain life and how messed up it can get if you are human. But then why crush her spirit.

First things first, call the doc's office and set the appointment. He felt confident it was not going to be good news. His arm did not get better for all the treatment and therapy sessions. That was what the doc would tell him when he went in. There is nothing we can do for you. Live with it! *I have been.* The bottle came up again, and a big gulp flooded his mouth.

Chapter Fourteen

1:15 P.M. Friday October 20, 1995

Art washed his face and checked for stubble. He picked up his comb and ran it through the hairs under his nose making sure they were uniform. Satisfied Art adjusted his sling and grabbed his car keys off the nightstand, turned and moved to the landing and trotted downstairs. Knowing his appointment with Doctor Spranger was in an hour, and the mystery about his arm and future would be solved, he rushed toward the garage.

The phone rang, and he stopped and turned to the sound. For a moment, he hesitated and then walked to the kitchen and lifted the earpiece. "Hello?"

"Hello! I am here with your daughter, Melissa. She's had an accident, and I have her in the backseat of my car. She insisted that I call you. I'm out on Turner Road, on the other side of Lower Sacramento Road by the canal. Do you know where that is?" The voice quieted and then rushed on, "She wants you to come. My car is by the oak tree on the dirt turn off. Can you come now? She wants you?"

Art gripped the earpiece hard, scribbling on his notepad. "I'm coming." He slammed the phone piece in its cradle and ripped the paper off the tablet. His thoughts of his arm and the doctor visit were suddenly gone. He rushed to the garage and didn't even reason to make sure the garage door closed before he left the driveway. All he could think about was getting to Melissa.

A red light on Ham and Turner Road got in his way, and he stared at it as though he had some power to make it turn green. He rocked his body to move the car forward. The passing vehicles seemed to be flowing by like thick honey. An eighteen-wheeler loomed in the roadway blocking his view. He tapped his foot, rubbed the steering wheel all to make the light turn green. It did, and he started up only to have a maverick car swing into a driveway at the shopping center. The immediate reaction had him stomping on the brake. Block by block he made his way to Lower Sacramento Road. The Wine and Roses sign caught his eye. Finally, Art freed himself of the urban area by crossing Lower Sacramento Road. He raced the car toward a road narrowing. The town drifted off behind him and was replaced by open country with its welcoming oak trees and green splashes of color backlighting a yellow and black guardrail that was meant to bring the traffic down from a three-lane roadway to one single directional lane.

Art grabbed the note up and tried to keep one eye on the road while making sure of the exact directions. There's the cell tower. It loomed over the oak tree, and the dirt circled off the blacktop and around the tree. If this is where the woman's waiting she'll be just behind that tree trunk. The slough ran to the left of the turnout and Art watched cars heading into Lodi for a chance to turn his vehicle off the road and into the pathway where Melissa waited in. *What was her condition? Why didn't I ask? Why didn't the lady take her to the hospital?*

Well, he couldn't ask that question now. This must be that nurse that Melissa's been taking care of her children. Melissa said something about her showing her things about the car, so she would not be so nervous. So, I will meet this nurse, something I should have done a long time ago.

Art saw an opening and swung his car across the yellow line and the oncoming traffic and to the dirt path that led to the tree and to the bumper of the dark blue older sedan. A 1998 Buick. Art turned his car off and left the keys dangling in the ignition switch and his car door open as he raced to the Buick. "Melissa?" He reached the open left rear door and slung himself into the interior of the car, "Mel?"

She was not there, just a blanket over some brown paper bags filled with newspaper. Art tore through them and was about the pull his body back out of the car when he felt a sharp pain.

Lifting his body, he banged his head on the door frame and blacked out. Coming to he realized someone had his belt and was shoving him forward head first into the interior of the car. He heard the car door close cramping his legs and he drifted, unable to keep his attention on what happened next.

Art blinked his eyes and realized that he'd been blindfolded. He twitched his eyebrow and used that muscle to move the material loosening it bit by bit. The car rocked and rolled over some country road. His mind would not clear, and he shook his head to try to make himself more aware. The lull of the road noise soothed him, and he drifted off.

85

Sometime later he blinked his eyes again under that blindfold. *What's happened that he was here like this?* A moment of fear flooded over him as he realized he was not in bed at home dreaming a nightmare. Little by little he worked at the covering, rubbing his head against the back seat to move the cloth to let him see. It seemed tight around his head, but just a slit appeared and allowed him a small view out of the car window. Tops of wooden telephone posts snapped by, one, two, three...he couldn't keep the count in his head. His brain was so messed up.

I must remember what I see. Country...Art slipped off to sleep again.

Art realized someone was guiding him out of the car, his head swam, and his stomach turned sick. He had trouble putting one foot before the other and the thought to leave this place crept in as things went dark again.

Some drumming sound entered his thinking, like a drop of water off in the distance. He blinked his eyes again. The blindfold remained in place, the slit gone. Art could tell he was not free to move around. His body was tied down to a cot. He could not move his arms or legs, and his only thought was on his pistol on his leg. *Was it there? How could he get loose? What time was it? What the hell happened?*

He tried to rub his leg against the confines. Fear choked him down. He could not move.

Art turned his head to the right and listened. The drumming sounded louder, so it was coming from that direction. There was water, and he could use a drink right now. His mouth felt cottony. He turned to the left and listened. Alone. That was the sense permeating his foggy mind. Art jerked his leg and the tie around his ankle pained him sharp and clear. A thought came to him that his left arm was not aching. He yawned and drifted back to sleep.

THE GENTLE GIANT RETURNS

Art woke with a start, aware someone stood by his side. The right side. He tried to form thought about this individual, to gather information about this person. Art shaped a word in his mouth to speak when a jab in his arm gave him all the information he needed. Someone drugged him. Why? And art drifted off.

Chapter Fifteen

Saturday morning, October 21, 1995

Melissa came downstairs yawning. She stopped and looked the room over. Stepping over to the coffee pot her hand wrapped around the glass base it felt cold. Her palm lingered a long moment as her mind took in the information. Her dad had not made coffee this morning. Strange.

She scowled at the appliance. No smell of morning breakfast met her nostrils. The kitchen remained quiet as though she was the first to enter. She yawned again and walked to the back door and opened it. Standing in the doorway, she listened to the pool filter cycle on and humming.

Daisy whined, and she turned to the cage and let the dog out. The pup raced to the door, and Melissa followed her outside. Melissa looked toward the dock and saw the red and white boat bobbing at its mooring. Her dad was not standing on the pier with a steaming mug in his hand, a sight she saw almost every morning from this doorway or the window of her bedroom, summer or winter. He loved his coffee and that river.

Melissa realized everything seemed too quiet. Her dad was nowhere. *He must be in bed still.* She watched Daisy working the ground over very carefully, not missing anything interesting to set her nose to. Finally, Daisy trotted to her and Melissa picked her up. "Hey little girl, did you have a nice morning in the yard?" She cuddled her, and they reentered the kitchen. Melissa put the pup down and opened the cupboard door and lifted the bag of dog food. She scooped a half cup and dropped it into the stainless-steel bowl, rinsed out the water dish and set it back down beside the food. Daisy eagerly ate.

When Daisy finished, Melissa took up the dish and washed it out. "Come on Daisy, let's go upstairs. Let's see if you can climb those stairs today." Daisy, always eager to please, jumped on Melissa's leg as she headed to the stairs. The pup threw her tiny body at the mountain facing her and managed two steps when Melissa grabbed her up and said, "Your legs will grow, you just wait."

Melissa walked into her room and set Daisy down and was about to take a shower when she turned around and walked out of her room to her dad's door. "Dad?"

No answer. Mclissa put her hand on the doorknob and waited a moment. "Dad?"

Still no answer. Melissa dropped her hand and went back to her room. With her ear pealed she stepped into her bathroom and dumped her clothing in a pile. She walked into the shower, her hand turned the faucet and set the temperature, she showered and then dressed. Melissa opened the drawer and pulled out her brush. *It's so short compared to the long strands I used to run the comb through.*

Melissa plucked Daisy up and placed her on her bed. She played with Daisy on top of her bed, and the pup made happy squealing noises. Realizing that her dad was sleeping right next door, she placed her hand over her mouth and stopped roughhousing with Daisy. "Shush, we don't want to wake Dad, he must be tired. Let's us go downstairs and get me some breakfast." Melissa yawned again. She felt tired from babysitting two nights in a row and was glad to have slept in her own bed last night.

It didn't dawn on her that when she came in so late last night that the house was quiet. She figured that her dad was out, probably with Amanda, and she got home before he did. They were living separate lives these days more and more. That was okay with her. She knew how happy he seemed with Amanda in his life. It made her glad to see he was pleased and not so upset all the time and on her case about being safe. How she hated that.

She knew he was trying to stay off her case but it didn't' need words, it didn't need anything but a look on his face or his eyes. She knew how he felt and she knew what he wanted to warn her about. But the lake had saved her, and she was feeling so much better.

If she admitted it, the reason she felt better was her mother. She brought balance to Melissa's life when there didn't seem any way to have balance. *Crazy as that woman seems to be. Well, crazy might not be the best word to describe my mother but she is off the wall about, well just about everything. Amanda, now she is level-headed, and she isn't scared. That's what my mother is. She's scared.* "What about? Huh*.*"

Daisy looked at her expectedly when she spoke. "Nothing, little girl, just thinking."

Melissa trotted down the stairs and into the kitchen holding the pup all the way. "There, we are all

90

cleaned up and ready for the day. I will be as soon as I get my breakfast."

The phone light on the recorder pulsated a steady red. Melissa pushed the button and heard Amanda's voice. "Art, pick up. It's me, pick up." The message clicked off.

Melissa stood looking at the phone a long moment, thoughts running through her head. *Was dad mad at Amanda? Did they have a fight? That just didn't seem right about those two. They always seemed to talk things through, and that was one thing Melissa liked and counted on. They were balanced. Why didn't dad pickup on her call?*

Her hand reached for and grabbed the cupboard knob, and she pulled the door open and lifted the box of cold cereal down. Melissa poured flakes out of the container and into a bowl. Her thoughts were on Amanda and Art Franklin. *What was going on and what should she do about it. And, what could she do about any of it?* She knew she wasn't going to let it go. *He never stayed out of anything concerning her life, and he was just as important to her as she was to him.* "Right? Right."

Her spoon dug into the breakfast, and without thinking about eating her food, she finished and rinsed the bowl. *I could go up and wake him up and ask him what's going on between him and Amanda. No. If he's tired, he needs sleep. I know he's been not sleeping that's because of his arm and because he's worried about me. I don't what him to worry about me.*

"Come on Daisy, let's go back outside. We need to figure this out together. Tell me what you think I should do?" The pup licked her cheek as the backdoor swung and slapped the frame. "Oh, that should wake dad." She put the pup down and let the goosebumps go away as she looked at his window. It remained still. *Boy, he must be out if that didn't wake him. That just doesn't seem like my dad. He usually is on any small sound he hears and runs to inspect whatever it was he heard.* She stood staring at the window as a decision surfaced in her mind.

Chapter Sixteen

1 P.M. Saturday, October 21, 1995

"**D**ad?" This time she opened the door and peeked inside. The covers were tossed over the bed as though to make it without smoothing everything in place. The pile of dirty clothes was shoved to the wall in the bathroom. He hadn't cleaned this room up yet today, and he's not here. *This is just strange. For him. Huh. He sure as heck wouldn't let me get away with this.* "Dad! Where are you?"

The room gave up no secrets, and she backed out of the space and went back downstairs. She looked up Amanda's number and listened as the phone rang. She was about to hang up when Amanda answered. "Art!"

"No, Amanda, it's me, Melissa." A streak of worry lit up the inside of Melissa's brain as she spoke. "Do you know where my dad is?"

The line went clear, and Melissa thought she'd lost Amanda.

"Amanda?"

"I'm here honey. I don't know where Art is. In fact, I have been trying to find him myself. We had a date last evening, and he didn't show or call. He let me sit it out in Pietro's. I can't get an answer on his phone, and I left a message on the house phone too."

A chill ran over Melissa's arms, "Well he's not home, and by the looks of it he hasn't been all night."

"He didn't tell you where he was going?"

Fear fed her, and she managed a shaky, "No."

That silence over the phone line happened again, and then Amanda spoke, "I'm coming over now, stay there and wait for me."

A feeling of relief flooded her as Melissa hung the phone up. How could she feel better and scared at the same time? She felt glad Amanda would come, but something was wrong. She had to figure this out, and she didn't know where to start. Melissa caught Daisy up and placed her back in the cage. "You stay there honey, out of the way and out from under my feet. You could trip me up, and I need to move right now." *Move where?* She turned right and left and couldn't think of one thing to do that would help her find her dad.

It took Amanda a long time to get from her place to Melissa, but it didn't matter, Melissa was standing in the doorway as Amanda came up the walk. Melissa's green pants and pullover shirt with green and white stripes looked crisp and fresh, a harsh contrast to the worry written over her face. Red and golden glints fired off her hair from the sun as she hurried to meet Amanda. They hugged, and Melissa allowed the woman's arms to encircle her and make a safe feeling fill her for a fleeting time. She backed away, and Amanda said for them to go into the house, so the neighbors wouldn't become interested.

They walked inside, and Melissa began to cry. "I don't think he was home since sometime yesterday. I babysat for Sharyl the last couple nights, and I came home when she got home from work last night. I was ready to sleep in my bed, and I didn't even check in with dad. I just went to bed."

"It's okay sweetheart, we will figure this out. Your Dad's not going to leave you, or me for that matter, without letting us know. The first place we'll check will be the hospital. Give me the phone book, and we will start calling."

Melissa had the book out of the drawer and Amanda grabbed it and flipped the pages to H. "Here," she snatched the phone by its body and pulled it toward her. "Let me call them."

She looked at Melissa as they waited for the hospital to answer.

"Memorial Hospital, Eleanor speaking. How may I help you?"

"Hello, Eleanor, I'd like to check to see if someone is in the hospital. Arthur Franklin. Is he there?"

"I'll check."

Amanda smiled at Melissa as she kept the phone to her ear.

"We have no one here by that name."

Amanda looked at Melissa and shook her head, "Can you check emergency? Could he be there, and you wouldn't know that?"

"Just a minute."

They waited, and the time seemed to drag when Amanda put her head and the earpiece closer together, "I see. Thank you."

She hung up. "He's not there. There are urgent care units all over town. Let's check them out. Amanda brought the phone from her ear, "They don't have him." She placed the phone back in its cradle and looked at Melissa. "You don't have any idea where he might have gone?"

Melissa shook her head and wiped a tear that refused to stay put with a jerk. "We've always told each other everything. Oh well, there's been times when I was mad at him, but we've always known how to find each other. I don't have a clue where he is or why we can't find him."

"Do you suppose your mom might know something?"

Melissa shrugged. "I was thinking, what would my Dad do right now. And I think he would be calling all my friends."

"Okay, so who would you call first?"

Melissa pointed to Amanda. "Well, right, but who else would be on the list?"

"Walt? Murphy and Yvonne. I think he's been spending time with them."

Melissa opened the phone book drawer and found Art's business phone list. She laid it on the countertop between them. "Everyone should be on here."

Amanda reached for it, and the two poured over the names, "Here, I'll call Walt, I have that number. And then we'll try Murphy." She dialed, and Walt answered right off.

"Art?" Walt said.

"Sorry, it's Amanda, and I am here with Melissa. We are looking for Art. Is he with you?"

Walt breathed into the phone and Amanda heard it was that kind of communication where you know in your bones that the other person has something important to say, but they don't want it getting out beyond the person listening. Amanda sliced her eyes at Melissa who waited with doe-like eyes for the answer. How should she proceed? "So, Art's not been there today? How about yesterday?"

"No. got a new crime scene on my hands. It's going to take a few hours. Why don't you come on in.?"

Amanda felt goosebumps race over her body.

"Talked to him yesterday morning, he was going to the docs. Get in here as soon as you can and leave Melissa out of the loop. Do what you have to do, get it?"

Amanda smiled, "Okay Walt just checking." She put the phone down and gave Melissa a worried but strong look. "They talked yesterday morning. Walt doesn't have anything else on him."

"I think I will run out to the place your Dad and I always meet and see if he's been there. Maybe someone has seen him. You could call Murphy and Yvonne and see what they know. Call anyone else you can think of, and your mother, I will be back as soon as I finish." Amanda wrapped her hand around her purse strap and pulled it to her, setting it over her shoulder. "You okay for a while?"

Melissa watched her leaving with mixed emotions. It just didn't feel right. They were making calls to find her dad and now, suddenly, Amanda's dropping out, dismissing her. Melissa would be alone hunting for her dad. Oh well, she sure has had her share of people dropping out on her and messing with her life. There's a lesson to be learned here — don't trust other people.

After the door closed on Amanda's car and it glided away from the curb Melissa returned to the phone and called dumb ole Murphy. What did her Dad see in him anyway? He had that crooked smile and that one front tooth that tilted off just a little. And he was always hanging around here. She sure hoped this call wouldn't have him running over here right now. That's the last thing she would need. She dialed and listened to the call go to voicemail. He's probably on shift. "Hi Murphy, It's Melissa, I am looking for my Dad and wondered if you've seen him yesterday or today?" She placed the earpiece back in the cradle

She stared at the phone wishing it to ring and that it be her Dad. It just sat mute. Her heart raced, and she reacted by finding something to chew on. Melissa pulled the bread from the refrigerator and picked a slice free from the loaf. *I guess I should call my mother. She'll come flying in and turn this house into a circus. We don't need that. What could she know about my dad anyway? It's not a good idea to bring her here especially with her and Amanda not liking each other.*

Her hand went toward the phone, and she lifted the receiver and punched in Yvonne's number. It was office hours still, so she expected the woman to answer. The phone just rang, and frustration built in Melissa. She took the phone from her ear and guided it back to its cradle.

"Hello?"

Melissa heard the voice and jerked the phone back to her ear. "Hello, this is Melissa Franklin. I am trying to find my dad. Has he been in today or yesterday?"

"No, he has not. I haven't seen him for about a week or more. I'll tell him you are looking for him if he shows up."

"Thank you." This was not going well. Then it dawned on her to check the garage for his car. She raced across the floor, grabbed the doorknob and jerked it open. The car was gone! *Find the car, and I find my Dad!*

Chapter Seventeen

1:30 P.M. Saturday, October 21, 1995

Shuffling feet, a cough off in the distance, phones ringing met Amanda as she walked into the Lodi Police Department and directly past the detective's station to Walt's office. Tracy moved toward her until she recognized that it was Amanda and she backed off and sat back at her desk.

"Walt!" She had hiked it as fast as she could to his office and managed a breathless. "What's up?" Shock struck her at the bags under his eyes and those orbs as dead as though without thought and feeling. It scared her just to look at him. He worked his mouth, but the lips didn't part. She wanted to shake him make him talk. Finally, he cast his gaze down, ran his hand through his hair and sighed. "We've got a body," slowly his eyes found hers, "in the lake." He looked back and forth in her eyes.

"Okay, what has it got to do with me, or . . . is it?" She couldn't let the words form. They ran around inside her mind. *Is it?*

His lips pressed hard together and turned white from the pressure. "I haven't seen the body yet, just a picture the cop snapped and brought back to me."

"Can I see it?"

Walt reached under the mat on the desk and pulled the picture into view. She took her breath, narrowed her eyes and stared at the photo. "Is it Art?"

They both were looking at the red hair and the similar body structure. The face was turned down into the water, and the shirt billowed with air above the body's surface. It could be Art's shirt. He wore blue a lot. Something about the hurt arm didn't look quite right to Amanda. "Where's the arm sling?"

Walt shook his head. "Don't know."

She trembled now, "Are they taking the body to the morgue?"

He nodded, "The coroner has been called, and he will go to the lake, and after he makes his determination the body will be moved. Then we'll know for sure."

Amanda's hands flew to her mouth and covered her lips. She stared at Walt.

"Sit down Amanda."

She did as Walt told her and let herself down into the old personnel chair that had been in Art's office from the beginning. It appeared scuffed and well used. The wheels still spun, and the chair shifted backward a bit as she sat.

"Watch it, that chair can leave you on the floor if you're not careful."

She managed to get it under control. "Walt, I don't know what to tell Melissa."

"Nothing yet." He smiled a sick grin. "Don't want to rain on her parade until I have to." Walt held up an empty mug, "Coffee?"

She shook her head. "Don't want the acid right now."

"Right, right. Me neither."

"How long's it going to be?"

"As long as it takes."

She stood, "I'm going out there. Maybe I can learn something."

Walt slung his hand up, "Don't do that."

Her hands flung out pleading, "I can't just do nothing. If it's Art — God, don't let it be — I need to know."

"What we are trying to do right now is keep this low key until after the coroner's been there and gone. Then we can get him out of there, and I'd like to do that without all of Lodi the wiser."

"Do you really think one more car driving into the park is going to make that much difference?"

"Yes, especially one with the driver heading straight for the crime scene. I am asking you to hold off."

"I can't leave Melissa alone at the house all by herself."

"Then go back, and I will come as soon as I know one way or the other."

She got up and headed out the door, turning to the left and crossing in front of everyone. Amanda kept her eyes forward and her mouth shut as she made her way back to her car. The door slammed shut and startled her. Her lip turned under, and she bit down until pain told her to let go. *What am I going to say to that child? Should I get, her mother to come. Or, should I wait until we know for sure?*

101

She started the car and drove it to Turner Road, slowing to look at the lake as she passed by. If there were any official cars there, she couldn't see them. They must be back around the riverside. The lake looked flat and a deep aspen green as though an artist had squeezed one shade out for the whole scene. No boats were sailing at the time, she couldn't see anyone walking around the lake. It felt as though no one was there. She managed to keep the wheel following the yellow line that held the two lanes apart. Amanda drove to the block that led to the street Art, and Melissa's house was on. She guided her car to a spot out front and saw Melissa watching out the front window. That lonesome look told the whole story. She had no new news about her dad. He was MIA.

I am going to call Jim and get him over here. Amanda left her car and walked to the front door. Melissa held it open and asked as soon as Amanda stepped across the threshold, "Did you learn anything?"

Now she was going to have to lie to the girl. That isn't how she wanted their relationship to begin. It was getting them off on the wrong foot right off the bat. *Walt wants to wait until he is sure, what do I do. Follow his lead and explain it to her later that I didn't want to worry her? She will never trust me. Going forward there will be a vast distance between us. I think I must tell her what we think might be happening.* She smiled at Melissa. "Very little. How about you?"

"I called Yvonne, but she didn't know anything." Melissa shrugged her shoulders. The two continued into the kitchen.

"Did you call your mother?"

Melissa shook her head.

"Why not?"

Melissa looked away, "Just didn't."

"Honey, sit down."

Melissa pulled a bar stool out and crawled up placing her elbows on the countertop. With a sad expression, she looked around the kitchen. It seemed like someone else's kitchen, missing the sounds and smells that were normal to them.

"Honey, I have something to tell you, and it's going to be hard to take and understand. I went to see Walt. A body has been found in the lake, and it appears that it could be your Dad. Until the coroner releases the body we are not going to know for sure. Walt didn't want to worry you, but I think you need to know so you can process all this. I want you to know we don't know for sure that the body is Art's it has red hair and a blue shirt. Do you know what he was wearing?"

Melissa trembled and began to cry deep sobs until she brought her arms on the counter in front of her and dropped her forehead onto the arms. She cried hard, and Amanda rubbed her back and shoulders.

"Honey, did you hear me. We don't know for sure. Let's not borrow trouble before it's here. Walt just wants to see for himself, and then he will come tell you. He promised."

Melissa pulled herself up from the counter and flung herself into Amanda's arms, sobbing.

"Awe, honey, I had to tell you. Please, let's just wait and see how things work out. You know Art could come walking through the door at any minute."

Crying a while longer Melissa slowly quieted. Sleepily she stared at Amanda. "I guess I have to call my mother. I thought you were going to be my mother." Her face screwed up, and the sobs began again.

"Maybe I shouldn't have told you. Walt wanted me to wait, but I thought you needed to know and you'd be upset if you found out later. I am sorry sweet girl, I am so sorry." She smoothed the hair back from Melissa's face and smiled at her. "Let's hold the good thought that the body is not Art's and that he will be coming home soon."

Melissa wiped her eyes. "Amanda!" She spoke with authority. "The river wouldn't take my Dad's life and save mine. It wouldn't. That's not my Dad." She sat back. Gazing down at the phone she pulled it over and punched in her Dad's cell number. It rang and rang and went to voicemail. "Where is he?"

"I wish I knew." Amanda smoothed the hair from her face again. "I am going to fix you and I some tea. We are going to be here a long time, I am calling Jim first, then I'll fix it."

"I'll do it." Melissa stood, "You don't know where everything is, and I do. So, you sit down and let the young one fix the tea." She moved as though in sleep, reaching for the teapot and the cozy. She filled the pot with hot tap water and set the cozy over it sliding it to the countertop. At the cabinet she lingered, fingering cans of tea, choosing Jasmine Pearl. "This has a one-minute steep time, and it is delicious." She worked, placing the filled pot on the stove and placing lovely teacups on matching saucers. "These are mine. My Dad gave them to me when I was a little girl." Her finger ran around on the rim of one of the cups. "He told me one day I would want to give a real tea party." She smiled and put out one more cup and saucer. "Just in case he shows up while we are having tea.

Chapter Eighteen

2 P.M. Saturday October 21, 1995

Amanda watched as Melissa moved with competence around the kitchen. She kept her eyes on the girl as she pulled the phone closer and dialed. A moment passed, then she said, "Hey, Jim? Have you seen Art?"

"No, not for a couple of days. Why?"

She observed the troubled girl as her quiet voice said, "Can you come over to Art's house now?"

The voice had a professional sound to it, and Jim responded. "Be right there."

Amanda put the phone back in place and put her hand on the girls warm back as she set napkins on the counter by the three cups and sat back on the stool. Even through the quiet steeliness of her body Amanda knew Melissa was grieving. From the history Art had told her about Melissa's ordeal, she knew this was just one more nail in the girl's emotional coffin. How much one young girl could be asked to endure was a mystery to her. If she could do anything to lessen the pain, she would. Should she fix her something to eat? Melissa's head was down on the counter again, and she breathed short quick lungsful.

In ten minutes Jim knocked on the side back door. Amanda walked over and unlatched the screen to let him inside.

"What's up?"

Amanda nodded toward Melissa and saw in Jim's expression that he could see the girl was in a sorry state. His eyes quizzed with wonder as they swung back at Amanda. His head bent toward her as she whispered, "Art is missing, and a body has been found at the lake. It could be Art. It has red hair and a blue shirt."

Jim's eyes widened and he nodded that he had the picture. He sighed deeply and walked over to the stool next to Melissa. He let his body down on the seat and brought his elbows up on the counter. "I'm here if you want to talk." Jim quieted and waited for her to acknowledge that he was there. He sat looking across the room and breathing deeply.

A long time passed with the only sound coming from the old kitchen clock on the stove clicking off another minute and another. Jim didn't move. Amanda watched. He was so good with hurting people, and she knew it. She prayed two prayers at the same time and smiled to herself. Who said women can't multi-task. One prayer was that Art was okay and would come walking in the door any minute. The other was that God wouldn't take both of them so far to dash their dreams of a life together. She felt guilty that her prayers were self-serving and not for this poor girl. Amanda could not help being about to dissolve into tears. Now that Jim was here she could turn to him. Amanda braced her back, she must be strong right now. Don't give in to the fear.

Melissa raised her head, the red face and swollen eyes told of her pain.

Jim grinned and then let his face become stern. "Melissa, hold onto whatever reserve you have. Your dad may need you to be strong right now. Let's use the fact that we know there's no bad news yet. Let's worry about bad news after we get it and not one minute before."

His face, now so close to hers, allowed only the nose, mouth and the chin in focus. They were filled with wrinkles and the beginning of a beard and she centered in on those hairs and signs of age. The lips moved as Jim spoke and she smiled to show she was listening and she nodded at him. "My dad and I have been through some nasty stuff, and we are okay now. I want to believe that he is coming home. That's not my dad in the river." Tears welled up as she shook her head. "The river saved me, and it would not take my dad, it wouldn't."

"You hang on to that thought." Jim turned to Amanda. "Amanda and I will be right here with you every minute. We won't leave you. You don't worry about anything. We will do that for you."

Melissa didn't know how to not worry, but it did feel good to have these two people here right now. She tried a weak smile for Jim, and it faded just as quick.

"Melissa, did Art say anything about where he was going yesterday or today?" Jim said.

"I talked with Walt, and he said Art was going to see the doctor." Amanda moved closer to the counter."

"Okay, let's start there." Jim's hand circled. "Where's his appointment book?"

Amanda looked around and back to Melissa. "Mel?"

"I think he keeps it in his pocket. I never paid any attention to any calendar of events for him. Maybe he's got something in the office."

They left the kitchen and walked together to the office only to find the door locked.

"Key?" Jim said.

"In his pocket. He didn't want me going in there while he was gone, so he's locked the door for years."

Jim nodded. "Do we wait for a while longer or do we call a locksmith?"

"Bust the door down. Let's get in there and see if Art's in there and he can't get up," Amanda said.

Just at the time the doorbell rang, and the three turned facing the door. They all could see the shadow of a man standing there through the frosted window. Melissa raced across the floor and flung the door open.

Murphy stood there in his uniform.

"Oh, it's you."

"Well, that makes me feel welcome. You tried to call me? I checked my messages and came over as soon as I got off."

Jim and Amanda spoke up at the same time. "Art is missing, and we can't get into his office. The doors locked."

Murphy's gaze swung past them to the office door, and he strolled across the floor, saying as he went, "You want the door open?"

"Yes" came from all three just as he raised his foot and kicked the door at the latch area. The door gave, and all four of them poured into the room. Empty of Art and anything that they could see that would tell them where he went or might go. Murphy pressed the button on the message machine, and they listened to the last few messages that had come in and not been deleted.

"He had an appointment with the doc. Let's call the office and see if he made the appointment and went to it."

Amanda turned to the door, "I'm going to look the number up in the phone book."

Melissa followed her to the kitchen and leaned close as Amanda found the number and called. The answer wasn't good. Art had the appointment at 1:45 p.m. and he was a no-show and didn't cancel.

"Where can he be?" Amanda's voice began to crack.

Melissa placed her hand on her arm, and the two looked at each other.

Amanda wrapped her arms around the girl and they hugged quiet and long as though they had lost something dear and would never get it back. She kissed the girl's head and squeezed her just before letting go and stepping away.

The two men joined them. "We didn't find anything in there." Jim said.

Melissa sat on the bar stool and looked from one to the next. The old people didn't know what to do. She had to think, what would Dad do? Get busy. Dad always said when the road gets hard to get working. She remembered being stuck in that dark basement and how scared she was and how she tried to get working but didn't know what to do. Or, if it was safe to move around. Could he be in some place like that right now and not know what to do? How can I help him? What can I do? I don't know what to do. She felt like dissolving into tears. Just looking at the faces around her scared her more. They didn't know what to do either.

Her bike waited on the side of the house, and she could just walk out of here and scout about on her own. *Where? I can't believe my dad would go off like this and never tell me he would be gone so long.* "Something's wrong. My Dad would not go off and not tell me his plans." *I wish I could drive.*

She ran to the garage to double check. "The garage is still empty, Dad took the car! Where's the car?"

"What?" Amanda asked her.

"I just wanted to recheck the garage. I don't know why, I checked it earlier, and the car was gone. I don't know."

"We do things like that when we are worried, just normal to do it." Amanda softened her eyes as she gazed at Melissa's face.

Murphy called Walt and told him he was at the house and they were looking for Art and his car. Walt put an A.P.B. out on the car, and they seemed satisfied with doing such a small thing.

"We'll find him," Jim said.

Melissa placed her head into her palms and rubbed back and forth, trying to ease the itchiness of her tears and the lack of activity. She needed to remember everything her dad told her. Maybe there was something in all of that she could use to find him now. The old people were working together and her sense of things as always divided her off from them.

She lifted the phone and called Sandy. "Hi. It's me." She turned from the three of them and dropped her head down as she told Sandy everything she knew. "No, don't come over here. I don't know how long I am going to be here." At that moment, she knew what she was going to do. "I'll call you later."

Chapter Nineteen

3:30 P.M. Saturday, October 21st, 1995

Amanda turned the burner off under the whistling teakettle, and Melissa stared at the blue flame glowing yellow at the tips as they died away. Her attention followed Amanda who carried the steaming pot to the cups and began filling them. Then she joined the men at the counter. All heads together about Art and that conversation didn't include Melissa.

Adults exclude kids. They do that and don't even realize that the kid gets it, that they are in the way, not needed or wanted. Their voices melded into a steady hum and Melissa stepped to the back door. She waited a moment then went out and unlocked her bike, pulling it off the wall-stand, all the while her attention held steady on the backdoor. No one seemed interested in what she did. She thought about saying bye, but why? She rolled her bike to the gate.

The old wood and hinges squeaked as she passed through and closed it behind her. Melissa waited to see if anyone would come to check out that noise. No one did.

Once at the street she slung her leg over the bar and found the petal with her foot. As she pressed down the bike rolled off, and the tires hummed over the blacktop grit. At the corner were two cars making a right turn, and she slid to a stop behind them, waiting to get onto Turner Road. Once they moved, she took her place and made a safe turn.

The street seemed extra busy now, and she did her best to stay out of the way of passing cars while going by parked vehicles. She passed houses appearing deserted at this time of day, their yards manicured and bordered by flowers. Some properties with flags flying caught her eye as she rode along.

Melissa let her foot down and stood at the Ham Lane light, waiting impatiently for the green. Crossing that street brought her closer to her intended destination. She could see the trees from where she pushed the bike. It wouldn't be long. Melissa's heart raced and her head pounded as she finished crossing the busy intersection, and she rode again. She didn't care what opposition she met when she got there, no one was going to stop her from her mission.

Reaching the edge of Lodi Lake, she got off her bike and rolled it up over the grassy knoll. Playground equipment had two little children and their mother in attendance as she wheeled her bike down the embankment. They turned and looked at her, and she waved and nodded back to them.

Almost to the driveway, Melissa listened to the sound of the lake, the ducks quacking and the leaves moving in the gentle breeze. Coming just this far from the busy road put her in a different ecosystem. She pushed harder, in a hurry now to get to the body. If it was her dad, she had to know. Melissa rode again across large roots as they pushed up through the blacktop surface, past the trees on one side and the houses on the other that lined the lake edge. She didn't know just where she would end up, but if that body was still there, she was going to find it.

A cop car would be nice, she reckoned, and one I can see right now. It didn't happen. She moved, circling the lake as she passed the gateway to the wilderness area. Melissa slowed, put her foot down and studied the roadway until it made its turn into the redwoods, then she looked into the hardwood forest as far as her eyes would go. No one seemed in any hurry to see anything, so the body was not that way. Nothing looked wrong. She knew there would be yellow tape bordering the limits of the crime scene. There didn't seem to be any yellow tape anywhere.

Did Amanda have it right? Was the body somewhere else? There's a whole river snaking east to west. That body could be anywhere. Melissa pushed off again and headed to the picnic area. There she could see the bumper of what she believed was a cop car. Riding that way as fast as she could pump had her heart racing. Reeds were piercing up from the lake surface. They seemed to race the other direction on her left as she rode along the painted curb on her right. She was out of breath by the time she slowed and came up behind the unit. The coroner's car was there too. That meant the body was still here. Why did she feel glad? She dropped her bike right behind the cop car and began peering every direction to get the lay of the land. She walked by all the personnel as though they were not there, heading for the edge of the lake and the boat launch pier. She walked along the floating boardwalk, looking into the water and the reeds.

"Hey, Melissa, what are you doing here?"

She hardly looked his way, knowing Detective Brodton when hearing his voice. She knew them all, and they better darn well know her and leave her the heck alone. If her dad were here, she would know that soon enough.

The detective came after her, walking faster to keep up. "Hey." He reached forward.

Melissa shrugged his fingers off her shoulder as quickly as they landed there and trudged onward. She saw the gurney off to the left and by an outhouse. Some trees obscured her view. It was enough to head her that direction. No one would halt her intent. She made for it as Brodton caught up, "Melissa, you shouldn't be here."

He could have been on the moon for all she cared. Her shoulder jerked away from his hand again, and he made a sound that let her know he was not happy with her. She made it to the gurney as a man zipped the body bag closed. His hand lifted, gliding the zipper over the face.

Melissa pushed harder to reach them, and she was rewarded with a glimpse of hair. It ran a chill up her spine. She saw red.

The red hair, soaked in lake water, stuck out of the body bag just enough to fill her with dread. She slung herself over the gurney, grabbing the body by the chest area and crying out.

Brodton's hand rested on her back as the sobs racked her body. "Melissa."

She cried.

"Melissa," he gently worked his hand under her waist and shoved his arm under her, lifting as he felt he had enough of her. She clung, and he pulled. The other officer came to his rescue and helped move her off the gurney and body bag. Melissa kicked and squirmed to get back there.

Detective Brodton pressed his lips hard into her hair close to her ear, "Melissa, listen to me."

"Leave me alone. That's my dad, not yours." She squirmed and fought hard. "Get your hands off me."

The other officer said. "Get her out of here. We are trying not to draw attention to the area. Walt's going to kick my ass, yours too, if we don't and soon."

"What the hell you do think I am trying to do? She's a hellcat. Can't you see that?" Brodton pulled, and she flew like a rag doll away from the body bag. Her arms and legs flayed in the air and she adding to the scramble by kicking anything and everything she could come in contact with. He growled at her, "Melissa, listen to me please." He softened his grip and his voice. "You've got to stop this and calm down. It's not your dad, it's not Art in that bag."

She stopped and turned to him, gazing deep into his eyes trying to believe those words. "It's not? Let me see."

Brodton nodded. "Let her see."

The other officer walked over to the gurney and Melissa and Brodton followed. He unzipped the bag over the body's face until she could see for herself. She leaned over and said, "Who is that?"

Chapter Twenty

4:05 P.M. Saturday, October 21ˢᵗ, 1995

Brodton held Melissa's hand more a grip then hand holding, and she followed him into the station and to her dad's office where Walt now worked. "Come in here and sit down," he said to her almost slinging her into the chair.

She plopped into the seat and looked at Walt with burning eyes.

He looked equally off guard. "What's this all about?" Walt said.

"She showed up at the crime scene and made drama."

Walt nodded, slid his gaze toward her.

There, on his face, she saw disgust. Was it pointed at her?

"Well, Mel, you must be relieved to know it's not Art."

"I am." She sat forward. "But, where is my dad?"

Walt's lips pressed hard together, and he shook his mop of hair ever so slightly. "When did you miss him first?"

She shrugged, "I guess this morning. When I got up, and he hadn't made coffee or any breakfast for himself. He usually does that. And he didn't let Daisy out. He always does that."

Brodton shifted from one foot to the other, "Are we going to start searching for Art?"

Walt allowed his voice to be soft and reassuring as he spoke. "Melissa, Brodton is going to drive you home. Rest assured your dad will be our top priority."

She'd been dismissed. That happened a lot these days. It was a royal pain in the ass, dismissal. He wasn't going to let her in on anything. Probably because he didn't know anything. Who's he trying to kid? Not me I hope. Walt's a good cop, a great detective, but he is only as good as his partnership with my dad, and he isn't here. I am not going to let them push me aside. I can run my own surveillance. I've been around this stuff all my life. I know it like the back of my hand. And no one is going to work like I will work to find my dad. "You're going to take me back to the lake, so I can get my bike. If it's still, there and not stolen on account of your strong arming me into the squad car and hauling me down here against my will."

Detective Brodton took a stance that read help me, *can you see what I am up against.* "See what I mean? Drama. I am only trying to help you, Melissa."

"Take her back to Lodi Lake and get her bike, put it in the car and take her home." Walt swung from Brodton to her, "And you stay put once you are home, Mel. Your dad will have my neck if I don't take care of you."

She knew that was right, but she had no intention of sitting it out like a good little girl, so she looked him in the eyes and failed to answer him. If her dad was in any kind of trouble like she had been in, she knew the faster he's found, the better.

She smiled at the two men knowing they would be put off, while her mind raced. What about his meds? Where are they? Does he have them with him? She had to get home and check them out. In her harried mind leads were forming and she wanted to follow them to the end. Melissa moved toward the door, "Well, are we going or not?"

Brodton followed her, and they walked briskly to the squad, and both got in, and the doors slammed at the same time. She was not about to let him open a door for her. He'd get the message if she had to keep giving it to him. The officer drove her to the spot where the bike landed. "It's not here!"

"Let's look around. Maybe they pushed it against a tree, or on the bike rack. Let's look. Okay?"

She wanted to scream. There wasn't time for this. She had to take time. They had to look. She needed her wheels. Especially now.

The radio broke the silence, and a static message began, and Brodton leaned over and paid attention to the transmission. "You hear that?"

"Yeah."

"We're going to your house; your bike will be there."

She pouted and crossed her arms over her chest. "No thanks to you."

"Melissa. Seatbelt!"

She uncrossed her arms and pulled the belt around her and clicked it into the latch. "There. Go."

As Brodton pulled up to the curb, the front door burst open and out poured Amanda, Jim, and Murphy.

"Where have you been?" Murphy said.

"We've been worried," Amanda said.

"You've got to let us know before you go off," Jim said.

Melissa gazed from one to the next. Their words were pouring forth like a waterfall roaring into her ears. Were they serious? They didn't even know she was on the planet, what, two hours ago? They were her dad times three. She shook her head in disbelief. God, can't they give her some room? She knew what she had to say so she did, "I'm sorry."

As Melissa got out of the car and Amanda reached her she wrapped her arms around Melissa's shoulders and turned her toward the house. They began to stroll that direction. "Aren't you relieved it's not your Dad." Amanda reached for the doorknob and turned it allowing it to swing open. "Walt just called and said you were coming home. We didn't know what to think when the police officer brought your bike back. We didn't know you were gone. Where did you go?"

"To the lake, I had to see for myself."

"Oh, honey. I'll go with you to do something like that. Right now, we need to know you are okay and safe." Amanda followed her to the kitchen, and they both scooted out a bar stool and sat facing each other. "Promise me you will let me know if you want to do something, please." Amanda studied her eyes intensely.

This was not a promise she wanted to make. She had to get upstairs and check out her dad's med supplies and decide if he had them with him or not. She needed to get moving, not sit here being told what she could not do like she was five years old.

"Promise me, Mel."

"Amanda, I don't know what I can or can't do right now. I have to find my Dad. I don't know what that's going to take so I don't know how to promise you I will stay put.

I will do this. I'll tell you everything I find out as I can. That's all the promise I can give right now."

Jim and Murphy stood five feet away. Murphy stepped closer to Melissa. "I will drive you anywhere you want to go." He turned to the others, "She's as smart as Art, and she's been watching him all her life. I'll bet if anyone can find Art she can."

Jim cleared his throat. "Murphy, you go against the department on this and you could lose your job. You willing to do that? Walt said to keep her here and safe."

Melissa stared at Murphy. He understood. The big, dumb guy understood. Who'd a thought? Her judgment of him took a turn for the kinder. Not a lot, but a little.

"My dad's been running scared since Ray McNamare came into our lives. He's scared of losing me, and now it looks like I've lost him. Someone was shooting at him, and he figured it was no big deal. Well, maybe it was a big deal. Has anyone checked out where the loony-tunes is right now and what he's doing?"

Jim and Amanda looked at each other. "Call Walt," Jim said.

The two moved towards the phone.

When they got off, they told her that Mac McNamare was on a fishing trip at Comanche Lake.

"How'd Walt know that, I wonder?"

"I don't know honey."

Melissa had to leave these three behind and get up her dad's room to find out about his meds. "I'm going to the bathroom." She started and walked away unfollowed. When she could she ran up the stairs and into her dad's bedroom. Where would he keep his meds? Peering around and in all the areas easy to view, and then Melissa walked into the bathroom. He didn't have anything in the medicine cabinet, nothing on the counter. She went to the bed stand and opened the drawer. His gun was gone. She knew he put his leg piece in that drawer. His meds were there all in a row, and Melissa couldn't tell when he'd taken any last. Not today for sure. She shook the pain med bottle and found it almost full. She put the meds back in place in the drawer and slid it closed. Melissa didn't discover anything helpful except he needed his medicine.

She went to the bathroom and flushed her toilet, then trotted back downstairs. Standing by the phone on the counter she noticed the notepad. Her dad had ripped the last note off leaving a bit of paper behind. She raised the pad and noticed some indentation on the paper. Melissa reached for a pencil. Carefully she placed the side of the lead on the paper and scrubbed back and forth until the words made sense.

"Melissa, Accident, Car, Turner, Canal." She couldn't understand what the words meant. Slowly she rose. Carrying the pad, she went to the others. "I've found something, and it's in Dad's handwriting."

They all looked at it and wondered out loud each with their own speculation.

Jim turned to Melissa, "Did you have an accident?"

"No." She shook her head. "I haven't begun my driving lessons yet."

"What car, what canal?" Murphy asked no one and everyone.

Amanda tapped the pad with her fingertip, "Turner must be someone's name."

"Or, Turner Road," Jim said.

Yeah, but what about it? Melissa supposed.

121

Chapter Twenty-One

5:10 P.M. Saturday, October 21ˢᵗ, 1995

"Hi Tracy, put me through to Walt." Murphy held the open line waiting for the answer. "Hello?"

"Walt, Murphy. I'm going to drive Melissa around. She's determined to look for Art. She knows you won't be looking for him before morning and she isn't going to wait. I can stick with her and keep her safe."

A grumbling sound started low and exploded into, "Like hell you are. I said she stays put, and I want her there at the house. Do... you... understand?"

Officer Murphy dropped his head and nodded to the floor. "I hear you."

"Do you understand."

"I understand."

"Put her on."

Murphy cowered from the phone and Melissa with his receding body. He held the phone earpiece toward Melissa who cringed away. The cop's hand shook the earpiece. Finally, he looked at her, his eyes first pleading then stern and he set his jawbone, jerking the piece toward her again, Murphy mouthed. "He wants to talk to you."

Melissa shook her head, set her chin high, and clasped her hands behind her back. After a spell, she dropped her head then her shoulders followed. Melissa took a step forward and reached for the phone. At that point she looked from each of them back to Murphy. Melissa bared her teeth, threatening him. As she seized the phone from him, her fingernails trailed over his wrist.

"Yeah, it's me." Heavy breathing drifted into Melissa's ear.

"And it better damn well be you if I call and want to talk with you about anything at any time. Do we understand each other Melissa?"

Melissa's mental picture of Walt set him in complete contrast to the man speaking to her now. Where was that old teddy bear of a man she'd known all her life? She set her jowl, "When are you going to look for my dad?"

He coughed and cleared his throat, "Melissa, you know how these things work. Settle down and let me do my job."

"When?"

"I can't tell you anything right now. You know that."

Her hand flew out from her body in gesture, "My dad didn't take his meds with him. Wherever he is, he doesn't have his pain pills. Yesterday he had a doc's appointment. He didn't keep it. My dad needs help now, not tomorrow, or when you get ready. Now." Melissa's legs were spread apart, her right hand still extended and the fingers spread as she threw the phone back to Murphy who almost caught the wildly flung missile. It clambered to the floor, bounced and fought the constraints of the cord. All of them stared at it and heard Walt loudmouth while Melissa paced the kitchen toward the back door. High tension filled the room as they listened to Walt bluster at her.

"I want to know you are safe Melissa. Just in case your dad's been targeted, and you might be as well. I want you safely at home. Now, do as I say. Or, I can just as easily haul you in here and sit your butt in one of the cells."

"Whoa!" Jim said, "he's threatening to jail her. Can he do that?"

Amanda nodded her head, "I think Art would be right behind him. Wanting to keep her safe and out of any trouble."

Melissa rolled her tongue around in her mouth in defiance. "Come on Murphy, I'm going on my bike, or in your car. I'm going, are you?"

The hollow echo of the yell had each of them looking at the earpiece. "Melissa, I hear you. Don't defy me," Walt said.

Walt continued to threaten, and the three looked up to Melissa.

"Melissa, Walt really wants you to stay home. I think you'd better think about what he's saying," Jim said as he reached down and picked up the phone.

Amanda had her hands up to her forehead, her blonde hair sailing back and forth. "Come with me, sweetheart." She took Melissa's hand gently in hers and walked her to the couch in the living room. "Honey I understand how you feel. I want to go find him too. I think the police are the best ones to do that."

"They aren't going to start until in the morning. Dad's not considered missing yet Amanda. And I haven't even made out a missing person's report, that's going to take time, time my dad may not have."

The girl's face had a steeliness and Amanda recognized it as Art's facial expression when she saw it, and she nodded. "I know you are a strong girl honey and you'll do everything you can to find him. I know that. All of us know that. You've got the strength of heart, and you'll go the distance. No doubt about it one bit. I think you might be afraid that you may lose him forever, and you are acting hastily to stomp on those fears by finding him. I understand that feeling. I've got some of that too. I'm scared that I may never see him again and I don't think I can stand that. So, couldn't we keep this vigil together and wait for him together?"

Melissa heard her plea and wanted to help her on some level, but her dad took the forefront of her driving desire to do something.

"Challenges come to us in life, honey, and we cope with them as best we can. We learn that when sad things happen to us, we won't break and fall apart, we will go on. While this situation demands a lot from you, it will pass, and you will go on," Amanda said.

"You sound like my dad. He always says things like that. Telling me to get busy if I'm bored, that I'm not paying enough attention to what's going on around me. I think you guys aren't paying enough attention. My dad is gone. He didn't go to the doctor's yesterday. He's talked about nothing else but getting his job back, and he knows it hinges on what the doctor determines." She pointed upstairs. "He hasn't taken his pain pills today because they are upstairs in the drawer. His leg gun is gone." An accusatory finger lifted and directed Amanda's attention toward the kitchen. "That note says loud and clear that he was called away from here yesterday before the doctor's appointment and he never made it because he couldn't." Melissa stood, "Come with us if you want, but I have to find my dad. I believe he's in trouble."

Amanda put her hands over her mouth and blew out a hot breath. What should she do?

Melissa moved toward the door, and Jim placed his hand on Murphy's arm. "I'll go with her. Walt can't fire me, but he can you, and I think he'll be mad enough to do it if you go with her. Even if you find Art, he'll have to fire you for blatant insubordination."

Murphy scratched his head, and Melissa looked at him like he was a piece of secondhand goods. "Are you coming?" she asked.

Jim stepped forward, "Let's go Melissa."

"Do whatever she says Jim. That girl knows how to find Art," Murphy called after them as they moved out the front door and peeled off to the left. "Now where's she going?"

"I don't know." Amanda stepped out onto the front porch with Murphy and watched Melissa, with Jim right behind, head over to the neighbor's. A woman bent over her roses with her back to Melissa and Jim.

"Agnes, Hi. This is Jim Wexford, my dad's friend. We want to borrow your car. Jim will drive, and we'll put gas back in."

"Where are you going with my car?"

"My dad is missing, and I want a car that no one will be looking for."

Agnes smiled at her. She lived next door to a cop and knew Art's ways and helped him catch the man that broke into the house some months back. "I see. Where did your dad go?"

"That's just it, Agnes, I don't know, but I am going to find him." She reached out with her hand, "Can I have the keys?"

"Sure, honey." She reached into her front pocket and brought forth a set of keys. "Let me get the key off this ring really quick."

Jim reached for it. "I can do it. This key?"

"Yes, that one." Jim slid his nail into the slot and circled the key off the loop. The key dropped free and into the palm of his hand. He handed the rest back to the woman.

"Come on." Melissa turned and started for the car.

"Thank you," Jim said to Agnus and hurried after Melissa. He got into the Buick and started it up. "Good. Tanks full." He smiled at Melissa, "Hope the gauge is working."

Melissa slipped down to the floorboards and told Jim to move them out of the neighborhood slowly. He did as she said with one eye on her and one on the road.

"What do you see?" she said.

"You cramped down there. Why are you doing that?"

"If we are lucky, we got Agnes' car before Walt got any eyes over here. Do you see any cop cars?"

"There's one turning off Turner Road heading this direction."

"Don't look at them just keep your head forward and drive slow like an old fogey."

"Olay, they are by. What now?"

"Keep going."

Chapter Twenty-Two

5:25 P.M. Saturday, October 21st, 1995

Jim stepped across Tango Investigations threshold right behind Melissa. She walked straight to Yvonne's desk and stood there until Yvonne put the newspaper down.

Melissa felt the stare go through her. No smile, no grin, no emotion. Yvonne just watched her.

"You look like Art Franklin. You Melissa?"

Melissa nodded. "My dad's missing and the missing persons won't go into effect until tomorrow morning. I don't intend to wait. You remember someone shot at him just a little while ago. I can't take any chances that he isn't in trouble and needs our help right now."

"What do you propose?"

"We find his car."

Yvonne brought her gaze down from the girl's face to her blotter. "How do you propose we do that?"

"We break this town into sections with as many people as you employ." She waved her hand between herself and Jim, "We'll take a section, and we all comb them right now."

"I see." Yvonne's fingers tripoded and a smile promised to break at the corners of her mouth. The girl amused her. She's so similar to her dad. He didn't amuse her, he…well never mind. "I hire one person, so that would be three of us searching a pretty big territory."

"Then we need to get started. Dad hasn't had his pills since yesterday."

"You sure about yesterday? That's when he went missing?"

Melissa's eyes went wide. "I don't know, I've not been home for two nights until last night."

"Why haven't you been home?"

"I am babysitting, and I stay the nights the nurse works until morning."

Yvonne picked up the phone and dialed out. When Lessie answered, she told her to come on into the office as soon as she could. Then she led Jim and Melissa into her private workplace where a map of Lodi took over one wall. "You take this section." Her hand swept south along the outer perimeter, down Lodi Avenue to Davis Road. "We will get all the rest. Stay in touch. Whoever locates the car first stays with it, and the rest come to that spot. Understood?"

"Understood." Both Jim and Melissa said.

"There's one more thing." Melissa brought the paper from her pocket and showed the highlighted letters to Yvonne. "My dad wrote this on his pad by his bed. I think it's a clue."

Yvonne looked at it. "There's a canal off Turner behind the housing section. It's near the Verizon tower." She held the paper and asked, "Did you have an accident?"

"No."

"We don't know when he wrote this. Could be a long time ago and it has nothing to do with now."

129

Melissa took the note back and folded it placing it in her pocket. "Just the same, Jim, I want to go there first and see if the car is there."

"Okay."

Lessie came and called out to them, Yvonne told her where they were, and she joined them.

"Hi."

In a few minutes, Lessie was brought up to speed. Yvonne would take the area bordered by Lodi Ave. Gould on the East and Davis to the West, Kettleman Lane to the south, leaving everything southward to Harney Lane to Lessie. And they seemed ready to deploy. Jim caught Yvonne's eye, and he mouthed, "How much?"

Yvonne shook her head, and mouthed back, "Nothing. Family!"

They all walked back to the office's entryway. As they walked Jim nodded and grinned. Lodi turned out to be just the town he wanted to be a part of. If he could only get his house done and not be flying off on outside distractions. He felt bad the moment he thought that. Art was a friend. He felt happy to be helping. And Art just might have the key to his property's history. Did someone die in his home? What does that dead bird have to do with anything? What was on that tape that might mean something. He had good cause to help find Art. Because it didn't look like he was going to have his house cleared without Art.

Melissa reached for Jim's hand, "Where were you just now?"

"Nowhere. Right here with all of you."

"It didn't look that way. You looked off into the distance like you were thinking of something. Was it about my dad?"

Jim shook his head, "Just thinking about something and it has nothing to do with this." He used his hands to indicate this place right now.

"Okay, in that case, let's take off and head for Turner Road."

"Do you have any idea where on Turner Road?"

"I do now. It's across Lower Sacramento Road, almost across from the Wine and Roses property."

Jim nodded that he understood where they were going. "We'll check in, what number do you want us to call?"

Lessie reached over on her desk and brought back some business cards. "Use this number. It's my cell, and I will keep in touch with Yvonne."

Melissa trotted back to Agnus' car and turned to look at Jim as he walked to the driver's side and got in and looked at her. "Where to first?"

She pointed. "Drive off this lot. You can only turn right here, it's one way and gets on Lockeford Street. Turn Left and go to California. We'll go over to Turner Road there." Melissa snapped her seat belt in place as the car started up. Soon they drove northbound on California and reached Turner. Due to heavy traffic, they waited their turn. Jim brought the car on to Turner Road heading west for Lower Sacramento Road where they waited for a red light. "We've got a lot of ground to cover, but I want to see this place just in case Dad did go there."

Jim nodded. The light turned green, and he crossed the street. "The Wine and Roses and it's across from this place?" He swiveled his neck to see. "There's nothing but lawn over there. No place to park a car."

Melissa's finger indicated down the road, and he drove on. "See that narrowing? It's going to be up there I think."

Lodi's road building crew had placed a guardrail to funnel the traffic on Turner Road from four lanes to two which continued on seven miles to the 5 freeway. Just across from that guardrail were the big tree, the dirt path turnoff, the canal, and the Verizon tower.

"I see it I think?"

"Turn in right there Jim and let me out."

She jumped out of the car and held her hand up to stop him from driving any further. She was all Nancy Drew. Her head down as she walked over the circular dirt roadway, Melissa moved around the tree and came back to the car on the driver side. She placed her arms on the open window and looked at Jim. "I can't tell if my dad's car was ever here. I don't know what his tread looks like. I never thought I would need to know that. Now I wonder how I can find that out?"

"Probably like everyone else's. Do you know where your dad buys his tires?"

"No."

"Well, that's now a mute question."

"What do you mean?"

"If you don't know where he buys his tires we can't ask what kind he might have on the car now from the dealership."

"We've got to find a receipt."

"If he files. Does he?"

"I don't know."

"Do you want to go look for it?"

She put her hands over her mouth and thought.

"Even if he was here and you could identify his exact tread, Art's car is not here now. What good would it do?"

Melissa opened the car and got back in. Tears welled up in her eyes, and she wiped them away.

"Where to?"

"Well, we didn't see his car along Turner Road to this point so let's go down Turner to Davis and come back up Lodi Avenue.

They drove along, watching for Art's car and taking side roads as far as they would take them and then returning to the beginning point. On they went until they reached the intersection of Davis and Sargent. They turned toward town and came along, looking into the vineyards at every opportunity.

"He wouldn't drive his car into a vineyard," Jim said.

"I don't think he would, but I don't want to miss something."

Coming back to town gave them many more places to look, including parking lots and driveways. Art's car didn't seem to be anyplace visible. They continued on to Cherokee and across, looking carefully along the buildings and parking places to Guild. They took all the side streets off Guild and returned to Guild. Art's car didn't show up. The trip took them back to Turner Road, and they turned west once more until they came to the Manufactured Home Park. They turned in first toward the river and circled down and around, coming back to the beginning. They went across the street and drove the roadway, looking into each parking slot of each home and all the guest parking sites. Turning back onto Turner Road, they headed for the frontage road and drove it from north to south to Lodi Ave and then they were on the cross-town streets. This took them over two hours at this point.

"I'm going to need a pit stop soon," Jim said, "and we'll need to fuel up, we're at half a tank."

"I want to call Lessie and find out if they've found anything."

"Wouldn't they have called?"

"Where could my dad be?"

Chapter Twenty-Three

6:15 P.M. Saturday, October 21st, 1995

Jim's eyes shot up. The cop car was on their bumper before Jim looked into his rearview mirror.

"Geeze!"

"What?" Melissa said, turning to Jim.

"We've got company."

"Dad?" She spun around. "Oh!"

"I have a hunch our hunting days are over." Jim pulled over to the side of the road, coming to a stop in back of some parked cars. The cop's car was in the driveway, but there was no other place to stop. Jim turned off the engine and sat back. The officer approached and asked to see his driver license and registration. He was very businesslike, and Jim complied. Melissa sat quietly in her seat and hoped, against all hope, that they were being stopped because of something Jim did and not that they were after her. The officer looked over the paperwork, leaned down, and looked at her.

She looked ahead.

"This doesn't appear to be your car," the officer said.

"No, I've borrowed it for the day."

"From whom?"

"I, ah, don't know." Jim laughed an embarrassed chuckle.

"Unhuh," the officer said. He leaned down, looked past Jim and said, "Melissa, Walt said he'd like to see you in his office right way."

She knew Officer Rick. Melissa knew them all. And they knew her.

Melissa looked the officer's direction and grinned and said, "Hi."

"Would you please step out of the car."

She began speaking to Officer Rick when the car door on her side opened, and she looked into the dark suit waiting for her. She unhooked her seatbelt and slid out of the car. Officer Kelly didn't smile, he pointed to the squad car. Melissa walked that direction. "I can go home. I'll go," she said.

"You won't be able to do that." Officer Kelly said.

She saw that Officer Rick had Jim out of the car and they were talking. Melissa watched Jim's hands go wide as though pleading. She saw him shake his head and she squinted her eyes trying to understand what was happening.

"Get in," Officer Kelly said as he opened the back door of the police unit.

"What's happening?" she said.

"Walt wants to see you, so we are taking you to him."

"Okay, and Jim?"

Officer Rick walked back to the squad car and called in a pickup order.

"You're impounding the car? How's he supposed to get home?" She tried to get out of the car, but the door wasn't functional. She beat her fist on the glass to get their attention. They ignored her. It pretty much ticked her off, and she yelled at them through the grate between the front seat and the back. They didn't respond.

Jim paced back and forth. He was not a happy man, and she knew that by how he walked. "Jim," she said as loud as she could.

He turned and held his hand out to her to motion "not now." What the heck is happening, she wondered. They sat on the side of the road for about ten minutes when a tow truck arrived and hooked up to Agnes' car. Soon it pulled away, and the two officers got into the squad, and Melissa saw Jim standing on the side of the road looking at her as she rode away. "Hey, you can't just leave him there. Why did you impound the car? What did we do wrong?"

They didn't answer her. She got no information until she was in front of Walt in the office at the department. Boy, was she ready to unload on him.

He ignored her, paying attention to some report on his desk. The pen in his hand tapped and tapped against his forehead, and he read on. She just about came unglued. "Uncle Walt?"

"Not yet."

After five of the most slugish minutes of her life passed, Walt looked up. There came no smile, no greeting, no pleasantries from him. The soft teddy bear of a man had changed into a hard-boiled man. She didn't think she liked this Walt.

"I am glad to see you in one piece. His eyes, hooded by the thick eyebrows, glowered with anger. "Pissed, that's what I am." His jaw raised, "That you didn't listen to me and follow my orders. You have been with the force since you were a baby, Mel and you know the rules are set in place for safety first and foremost." He rose, the rumpled pants draped to the floor covering his shoes. The button on the top of his shirt was open, and his T-shirt peeked through.

She wanted to go to him and give him a hug, but something about him made her stay put in the chair. A chill raced over her. Did he know something about her Dad? *Get to it, Walt. Tell me.* She watched him, his face. The lines were for her a barometer. Maybe she could tell what he was thinking. She'd done it so many times before, right there in the kitchen of their home. Today the lines were no help. Walt came to the other personnel chair and sat across from her. It scared her a little. Nothing about Walt seemed reasonable or safe. He acted mad. Why should he be mad? She had a perfect right to look for her dad and no one, not even Uncle Walt was going to tell her different.

"Melissa. I need your help."

That shocked her, pupils popped as she answered, "Sure, what can I do?"

"You can go against yourself and do what I've asked you to do. Stay home and wait for me to find your dad."

Her shoulders dropped. "I can't."

"Honey," his voice softened like it used to do. "The car's been located. It was abandoned in a vineyard on Peltier Road."

"Abandoned? Dad's not with it?"

"No."

"Do you know where Dad is?"

"Not yet."

"So, you know something."

Walt shook his head.

137

"Are you looking for him?"

"I have been, not officially, but on my own."

"I am getting scared. My father's never done anything like this before. He always talks to me every night. They told me the guy that was shooting at him a few weeks ago was on a fishing trip at Comanche Lake. Is that true? Have you checked on him?"

"That's the first person I thought of. He's with another fellow, and they have been out there for four days now. He's not our guy."

"Couldn't he have done something and then gone fishing? Would he have taken my dad out there?"

Walt looked at the floor. Shook his head. "Listen, Melissa. I am this close to putting you in a cell and letting you sit it out where I know you will be safe until we find your dad." He steadied his gaze on hers. "I will let you go home on one condition. You call me every half hour and let me know where you are and what you are doing. It's going to register on my answering machine. If the call doesn't come from the phone at your house and from you, I will have you brought in here, and you will sit it out in a general population holding cell."

"All night long?"

"All night long! You'd better learn to cat nap."

"Come on, that's not human."

"That's the way it's going to be or the private cell. I'll let you pick."

Chapter Twenty-Four

6:30 P.M. Saturday, October 21st, 1995

Melissa stepped out of the squad car, her cheeks flaming, the breath forcing her nostrils wide as she strode up the walk to her front door. It swung open before her hand could clasp the handle. They spoke at once, and she looked past everyone but centered on Jim. "What happened to you?"

He smiled and shook his head. "Nothing to be worried about. They punished me for taking you in Agnes' car. They treated it as a stolen car."

"Does Agnes know?"

"Yes, honey, we've started bailing it out. Agnus will have her car soon."

"Crap. I can just guess what my dad will say about this."

"What happened at the station?" Jim asked, and they all circled around and walked with her to the kitchen.

"Walt said I could decide where I wanted to wait out the time it took the department to find my dad, at home or in a cell. I chose home. But. I have to call in on that phone every half hour. He's got a cop monitoring the answering machine, and if it's not that exact phone and me calling, then it's back to the station and a cell. My head's pounding. I need soda." She opened the refrigerator door and snagged a red can from the shelf. "What I want to know is...How'd the cops get on to Agnes' car?"

Murphy dropped his head, "That would be me."

Exasperation got the best of Melissa. Her face displayed her innermost thoughts. She hissed out, "You creep!"

He shrugged his shoulders and backed away from her. She rushed across the floor, soda in one hand, and pushed him in the chest with the other. "What is wrong with you?"

"I did my job."

"Get out! I don't want you here anymore."

"Melissa, you don't mean that," Amanda said.

"Get out. Get out...now!"

Murphy looked at her, gazed at the others and started for the front door.

"Don't ever come back."

"Melissa, he's our link with the department. We hear almost as soon as they do because of him." Amanda said.

"I don't want him here." She followed him to the door and locked it as soon as he was out of the house. "He's a plant. To know what we are thinking up. That's all he was. The creep." She watched as Murphy got into his car and sat there. "He's not leaving. Shit! Walt's put him on me."

"So, the car has been found and your dad's not with it. So…how did the car get in the field?" Jim asked.

"That's what we were talking about when you came home. Murphy told us the car was in a vineyard on Peltier Road."

"Yeah, that's what Walt told me. Why would my dad drive his car into a vineyard?"

"He wouldn't," Jim said. "Unless he was forced."

"Cheese! We've got to call Lessie and Yvonne. They are still looking for Dad's car."

"Right," Jim pulled the card Lessie gave him out of his pocket. Just as he reached for the phone, Melissa cut him off.

"Sorry, but my first call in is due now." She dialed and listened to the machine message. In monotone she said, "This is Melissa Franklin checking in. It's 6:55 p.m." She hung up and moved away from the phone and let Jim make the call.

After he told Lessie, Amanda asked them if they were ready for lunch. She busied herself fixing sandwiches and iced tea. They ate in silence, deep in their individual thoughts until the doorbell broke in. Lessie and Yvonne entered, and Amanda set more food and poured them iced teas. They all talked, and soon Melissa made her second call.

"He's got you tied to that phone," Yvonne said. "What we need to do is find Art."

"How?"

"That I don't know right now." Lessie wiped her hands and mouth with her napkin. "But sitting here on my butt isn't getting anything done."

"Let me see that note again Melissa," Yvonne said.

141

Melissa gave it to her and both Lessie and she huddled over it for a few minutes. "Okay, let's say someone calls here before his appointment with the doc and tells him Melissa's had an accident. He'd go. Say the place is by that canal on Turner Road by the big oak tree."

"We were there. There was nothing," Jim said.

"Doesn't mean he wasn't there. What day would that have been?" Lessie said.

"Two days ago. That's when he had the appointment with the doc," Melissa said.

"Someone lured him out there, and they took the car and dumped it in the vineyard. Who and why?" Yvonne said.

"We have to figure out who has an ax to grind with Art," Jim said.

"Can I have another ice tea to take with me?" Lessie said.

"Where are you going?"

"I am not getting anything done here. Out there I might."

Amanda poured her a drink in a cup with a lid and handed it to her. Yvonne followed her to the door. "What are you thinking?"

"I'm going to pay Mac McNamare a visit. Let's see what he knows."

"Keep in touch."

"Will do." With Lessie's usual flare she waved to Murphy and got into her car and drove off.

Melissa watched, and Murphy was on his radio faster than a flea could find a dog. "Creep. He's telling that Lessie was here and has left. Bet you anything Walt puts a man on her." She shook her head in disbelief. "How's he going to find my dad? Doesn't he know we are looking for him too?"

" Honey," Amanda said, "I think Walt is anxious about you. He thinks that someone has your father and that they may be after you. He's genuinely worried about your safety. I think you could help things along if you'd talk with him and assure him you understand and you won't cause him any more worry. Tell him you will stay with Jim and me the whole time right here at the house."

Melissa couldn't do that. She didn't know what she was going to do next. She hadn't figured that out yet, all except one part. The phone. Melissa had that figured out on the ride home and just needed the time to put her plan in place. She smiled at Amanda, not wanting to disappoint her. That was a moot point, she was going to disappoint everyone. It was just a matter of time.

Melissa had to shake them all, and the creep out front. Amanda wanted an answer, and she needed to give her one. She couldn't. Not the answer they all wanted. Time was ticking away. What could she do?

"Melissa, it's almost time for your next call."

"Call Walt and tell him you'll comply." Amanda pleaded with her eyes. Melissa stood and started for the kitchen and the phone. Amanda walked with her. "Call him sweetheart and get him off your back."

Her voice was flat and bored. "I'll call Walt, but I don't think he's going to give up on the phone thing unless I am in the cell. Because he wants me to call all night. It makes me think he wants me in that cell. And that I'll put myself there when I get so tired I nod off, and he can send a car to pick me up."

"That's downright diabolical," Amanda said.

"Well, how do you think the police get things done. They trick people."

"You don't believe, that do you?"

"Yeah. It's been the way it's worked around here all my life."

Chapter Twenty-Five

7:05 P.M. Saturday, October 21st, 1995

Murphy knocked on the door. Amanda answered and grinned at him. "How's Siberia?"

"I need to pee. Any chance I can come in for a minute?"

Amanda stepped back from the door. "Melissa's upstairs. You can use the powder room, but be quick. She's not happy with you right now."

"I know, but it's for her own good." Murphy moved past her and headed for the powder room.

Amanda went into the kitchen and poured a cup of coffee into a mug and walked back to the front door waiting for Murphy. He came and took the mug she offered. "Are you trying to get me back in here?"

Amanda shook her head. "She won't mind you using the bathroom, not really. Right now, buddy, you are out of here."

Murphy sipped, raised his brows, tilted his head and grinned a crooked smile, "Win some lose some," and he walked back outside. As he did something caught his eye. It was fleeting, and it was lost just as fast. When he got back into his car, he radioed for a replacement, and it wasn't long before another unit came and parked in Murphy's place. Murphy put the hot coffee in the holder and drove off.

If he could stay ahead of Melissa, he needed another set of wheels. A car no one around here knew. He contacted Willy and asked to use her car, an older Chevrolet sedan. Glad to loan the car to him, she told him he may need to have it washed as it has been sitting for a long time. *Oh, no*, he thought, *will the battery be up?* He would find that out when he got over to her house. Murphy completely repaired Willy's home and made it even better with his capable hands after Mr. McNamare damaged it so bad. The two bonded and it worked well for both. Wilma Concord, a 95-year-old widow and victim of that horrible man got a grandson in Murphy. And Murphy got a grandmother to bake him cookies and look after the bachelor.

Murphy made sure no one followed him to Willy's home. He parked his car on the curb and walked up the walk to Willy, who sat in the rocker on her porch. Her geraniums showed mostly leaves this time of the year with a few blossoms pushing color through.

"Here are my keys."

"Thank you. How have you been?"

"Just fine. When are you coming over for cookies?"

Murphy rubbed his tummy, "I'm ready right now."

"You mean that? I've got some ready to go into the oven, I'll get them going. Want some coffee or tea?"

M.L. WEATHERINGTON

"Wish I could, but I'm on stakeout right now. That's why I need your car. The person I'm after knows my car."

Willy smiled at him as though she were in the know. "Can't wait to hear all about this one."

Murphy stepped back, "I'll tell you everything once it's all tied up."

She smiled at him and waved goodbye.

He nodded and signaled with his fingers, got into her car and turned the engine over. It caught, and he pulled it out of the carport. Backing it he tapped the horn. Once on the road he made his way to the McNamare property. Passing, he noticed the garage door open and it empty. No one appeared to be home. He thought to run out to Comanche Lake and see if he could find Mac McNamare and just see what he was doing, and the more he thought about it, the more he wanted to do that. Walt had said to do what seemed right. He meant to go by his gut.

His mind raced this way and that. What did he see while he held that mug of coffee on the Franklin porch? Whatever, he didn't get enough of it to know. He didn't want to lose that piece of information by flying off the handle and going to see Comanche Lake, just to make sure Mac was in fact there fishing. *It's a big lake, and I'd need a boat to find him. No one fishes off the shore, except little kids.*

A flash caught his eye. *What was it I saw? Something, a color. That's it. I saw a color and that color did what? What importance does the color have? Someone went down the side of the house. Someone went into the Franklin house. I've got to get back there and check that out. If I call, they will tell me if anyone came into the house.* Murphy stopped and made the call.

Jim answered and told him a friend of Melissa's came over, Sandy, he said, and went on to say that Melissa had made all her calls, and the girls were upstairs right now. They took the kitchen phone up there and plugged it in. Jim told him he used Art's office phone to answer his call.

Murphy knew Melissa was up to something but didn't know what. He called the cop on duty out front of the Franklins and told him to be at the ready. Melissa may be working on making a break.

He decided to run out to the lake and check the old man out and then he should get some shut eye as Art and Melissa were priorities now. He swung the old Chevy onto East 12, passing the restaurant and the onramp to the 99-south freeway. He went by the gas station and about that time the lightbulb went off and the old Chevy's tires squealed in the tight turn the steering wheel demanded. How dense could he be? He shook his head at his stupidity and pressed the accelerator harder.

The light turned green on Cherokee Lane, and his left turn went well, taking over two lanes until he steered into the right-hand lane heading for the Turner Road ramp. All systems were go as he raced for the Franklin residence. If he was right! He'd soon know.

He parked the car enough down the street, but with a perfect view of the Franklin property. The cop car remained out front. The house looked quiet and peaceful. *Bet its anything but calm inside.*

Murphy checked the time, and when he looked up the front door opened. He smiled and watched. Two young girls, one Melissa and the other her best friend Sandy, came out of the house and walked to the side of the property. The blonde picked up a bike and turned it into the street. The girls talked a bit and then the blonde rode away.

Murphy grinned, "You're so busted." There was no one to hear him. He didn't care. The blonde rode past him, and he watched the other girl go into the house. He started the car and followed until the blonde stopped at the red light. He drove up beside her and said, "Melissa, did you really think you'd get away that easy?"

Melissa showed shock when he addressed her. He got out of his car and walked around to her, placed his hand on the handlebar and said. "Busted."

"Why are you calling me Melissa?"

He reached over and lifted the blonde wig over her head, exposing her red hair and her ire. "Because you are Melissa."

"I hate you Murphy, and I will for as long as I live."

"Tell it to Walt. He's waiting for you."

"No. You can't. I've got to get to my dad."

"Do you know where he is?"

"Not yet."

"You have some way of finding out?"

"I will."

"Where were you going?"

"I was going to the Lake to see if I could get some inspiration."

"Well, I think you're going to have to get your inspiration in a cell of Walt's choosing."

She pulled back, and he almost missed his chance to lock her down. They scuffled. Her arm sailed out and up bringing her elbow into his rib cage. He let a gasp out and grabbed her by her hair. So short now, but enough. Her head came back, and he managed to cuff her and put her in the back of Willy's car. He shoved the bike into the trunk and listened to a barrage of hate language as they rode to the station.

When they arrived, Melissa, too angry to cry. She glared at him, her hate for him growing by the minute.

Walt met them in the parking lot. Melissa came out of the back with her hands behind her back.

"Uncle, get me out of this."

"Not so fast." He walked beside her and slipped his hand around her elbow and directed her toward the building.

"You're not serious."

"You don't seem to believe me. I am looking for your dad. You are my first priority. To keep you safe and to find him. I have nothing else on my mind. And, yes, I am serious."

They walked through the department and to the back, where all the beautiful building materials disappeared, and block walls were everywhere. A solid door with a small window eye height faced her. There lingered a stillness as though life didn't exist here. An officer opened the door, and she felt shoved by Walt into the room. The floor scooped down with a drain in the center, so when they hosed this area down, it could flow out. There waited a cement slab to sit and lay on. Walt undid the cuffs. He stepped backward and through the door grabbing the handle.

It moved.

"Uncle. Don't leave me here."

Walt looked at her a long sobering moment. "Sorry, Melissa."

The heavy door closed between them and her heart pounded.

Outside the evening darkened against the day keeping its secrets.

Chapter Twenty-Six

7:25 P.M. Saturday, October 21ˢᵗ, 1995

"I'm Officer Green, Ma-am. I just came up the walk and rang the bell…"

"You need the bathroom?" Amanda stepped back so the man could come inside.

"No Ma'am. I came to tell you that Melissa's at the station and will be staying there tonight. I am going to leave now. If you need any further assistance or more information you can call the department at this number." He handed her a business card, smiled and backed away from the door.

Amanda closed the door, looked at the card and walked back to the kitchen where Jim sipped on his umpteenth cup of coffee. "That was the cop out front. He said Melissa's at the department and will be staying there tonight."

"What? I thought she went upstairs." Jim put his cup down, narrowed his eyes and said, "We've been played. Come on."

They tapped at Melissa's door, and the door swung allowing a one-eyed crack to open, enough exposed that they could see a form on the bed. Music played, and it looked normal. They both pushed the door open and thought it interesting that the girl on the bed did not turn around. "Melissa, how's it going?"

The girl turned and smiled. The scarf over her head hid most the blonde hair. "Sandy?"

Sandy explained her job for the time being. She pushed the button on the recording machine and played Melissa's voice saying that she checked in on time. She explained Melissa went to find her dad.

They called a cab and sent Sandy home and talked awhile about staying or leaving. Both decided they were tired and drained. Amanda wanted to get home, shower and sleep. Jim wanted the same. They cleaned up the kitchen, called the department and made sure Melissa would be there for the night, then told them they were locking the Franklin home up and could be reached at their homes.

They were at the door when Amanda said, "We've been so busy we forgot the pup, Daisy. She's been in the cage all this time. I can't take her. What are we going to do?"

They walked back into the kitchen and took the pup out of the cage and to the back door. Out Daisy pranced and did her business. Jim decided that he could take her for the night. He kind of liked the little thing anyway. Amanda gathered her food and water dishes, the dog food, and a bag of treats. Jim had his arms loaded down with the pup and a plastic bag of those items. He decided to leave the cage and get it tomorrow if necessary. They both thought everything would sort out in the light of day.

After the door was locked Amanda helped Jim into his car.

"You going to be able to sleep?" Jim said.

"I don't know. I feel sad for Melissa. She must think none of us are trying to find Art, or help her. She must be scared right now. There's nothing I can think of to do that will make any difference one way or the other. On the other note, I do not understand Art at all. He has been forthcoming and eager in our relationship. Why hasn't he called and told me what's going on? Do you think Melissa is right? That he's in some kind of trouble and can't call?" She yawned. "I am scared, Jim, that I might not ever see him again."

Jim kept his head down as he listened to her. Truth be known, he didn't know what to do. None of his experiences in life fit him for what should be done. If the police didn't know what to do, how could he? He felt drained and needing sleep, and if he went home and got some rest maybe he could come up with something helpful. "I think we should try to see Melissa in the morning and make sure she is okay."

"Do you think we should have done that tonight?"

Jim shook his head, "I think Walt warned her, and he is looking out for her safety, and he wouldn't do anything to harm her."

"I hope your right. I hope Melissa has a decent bed to sleep on. I know she's tired. She hasn't slept since deciding Art's missing. Okay, Jim. I'll say goodnight and see you, say 8 a.m. at the coffee shop on Lockeford, the one across from the old Sell Rite Market." Amanda reached into the car window and petted Daisy's head. The pup played happily in Jim's big hand.

She watched him drive off and sat in her car. Melissa could be in trouble, she thought. Her history of fear of being confined might get triggered. It's been good for her the last few months. I've got to be sure she is alright about this staying at the station thing,

Amanda started her car and headed for the police station. When she arrived, she found that Walt had gone home, as had most the day people. Amanda spoke to the custodian and got permission to talk to Melissa. She found her upset and frustrated, but not scared. That worked in her favor as far as mental health went. Amanda couldn't let the girl stay alone through the night in that icebox of a cell. That's inhuman. She found the custodian and asked to be connected with Walt. He came on the line, and she told him of her fears concerning retriggering Melissa's fears of confinement and dark places. Walt explained that the light in her cell burned all night so she wouldn't be in the dark. After many conversations, he did allow Melissa and Amanda to share an interrogation room together. It boasted two wooden chairs and a scratched-up table, four walls, and one door. They sat all night talking and waiting out Melissa's freedom.

"We are on our way Daisy. You are going to have this old man to sleep with tonight. I know you are used to Melissa." She licked his cheek. Jim drove into his garage and hefted all Daisy's stuff and the pup and closed the garage door. He went to the house and left the lights off. Enough night illumination followed him up the stairs and into his room. He closed the door so Daisy couldn't have run of the house if she got down. Jim went about fixing some water and a little food for the pup. Daisy had other interests, and so he picked her up and stretched out on the bed. Before long Daisy snuggled by his chin and Jim, let his body relax one muscle group at a time until cradled by the mattress. As stirred up about Art as he felt he still wondered fleetingly why he could go off to sleep so quickly.

He'd been asleep for several minutes when he awoke to Daisy growling. He could feel her throat trembling with the sound. Jim sharpened his ears and tried to locate the point of Daisy's concern. He didn't hear anything, deciding that the pup didn't know her new digs all that well and she probably listened to the house settle.

Jim let it go and turned, bringing his left leg up, Daisy cuddled closer, and the two drifted off again. This time Daisy woke him standing on his arm. She stared at the wall where an old painting hung. Jim tried to change her viewpoint, tried petting her, the pup would have none of it. Daisy walked to the edge of the bed and considered jumping down, but in the dark, it looked too far for her and she whined as she paced.

Jim figured the pup needed to go out. He just didn't want to get up, so he figured she could wait till morning. Daisy finally gave it all up and found a place to sleep. In the morning, when allowed down to get a drink or some food, Daisy raced to the wall under the painting and began digging frantically with her front paws.

She wasn't planning to stop digging at the wall anytime soon, Jim saw, so he picked her up and took her outside. The morning chill brushed his face and made him smile. "You find a place Daisy and do it quickly." She did and that pleased Jim who scooped her up and headed back inside. "I've got to get a shower and meet Amanda by 8 a.m." He placed her on the bed and then thought how he wished he'd brought the cage. After some more thought, he decided to take her into the bathroom while he showered. As he gathered a fresh towel and washcloth, he watched Daisy head for the spot on the wall again, and she frantically used her front paws to dig, whining the whole while. Jim started to say something but walked over to her, and as he did, he got a fear chill that raced over his body. Something bothered him. A cold, stabbing fear like fright-night at Halloween when he was a kid. Jim stood looking at the wall. He placed his ear to it and listened as someone breathed. Startled, he backed away, his eyes widening. Did he hear what he thought he heard? He moved closer to the partition. Daisy kept digging and continued whining and he pressed his ear again to the wall. This time he heard a shuffling sound, like a foot movement and a hand brushing the wall from the other side.

Jim ran his hand over the wallpaper, feeling for any uneven spots. Any doorways. Or sliding walls. Anything that would explain what he heard and that it was backed up by Daisy's response. Something lingered on the other side of the wall, and he had to make sure it wasn't rats. Jim took the painting down, and more chills ran over his arms. The picture of a dog had its eyes cut out, and someone could have been looking through them and watching him because the wall had a hole large enough for a full face to fit. What a crazy house this place has turned out to be. Jim tried to see in the hole, but it remained two inches too high for his legs to stretch. He ran his hand up to the picture holder that waited for the picture to be rehung. When Jim touched it something slid, and Jim saw the wall give. He stopped and ran his hand into the crack, pulling to the side. He knew immediately that he'd not make breakfast this morning with Amanda.

Chapter Twenty-Seven

6:15 A.M. Sunday October 22, 1995

Jim's hand pulled hard at the opened wall. It wouldn't slide any more than an inch. After a moment of checking everything out from every angle, Jim took hold of the hanger again, and the wall opened. *That's strange,* he thought. But once standing in the narrow hallway, Jim could see that the holder had a section on the inside of the wall, and the opening could be controlled by whoever had their hand on the handle.

The studs were not that old. It looked to Jim that the wood was reclaimed from some other project and used here. Knowing his carpentry as he did, someone had built this wall on purpose. When? His hand scaled over the stud nearest to him as he cast his eye the length. Someone knew what they were doing.

Okay, there're false walls, hidden passageways, secret entries, possible graves. What else can this place turn up? Rooms that I don't know about. People I don't know about? Who are they?

Jim so wanted to show this to Art. *He'd have to let the police know*, he guessed. Then reconsidered. *Well, maybe not. If there's no crime there's no reason to tell them What about someone watching me sleep. Isn't that a crime? I mean, they are in my house against my will, going around in areas I didn't know existed. Who does that? How do I prove it?* Sounds a little paranoid even to me.

"Hey!"

Daisy whipped around the opening, and Jim spotted her just in time. The pup could easily maneuver, but Jim's big burly body rubbed the walls. It acted as velcro pulling the shirt and pants material equally, while she scooted along unobstructed. "Daisy?" He called and kept moving her direction. She'd run out of sight from him but kept him informed with her bark.

He made it to the corner on the wall and just about turned back thinking he couldn't get his body through the small opening when something shifted, and he squirted past the narrow spot and found the new area a bit larger and more accommodating. Daisy kept up her woof, and he felt like the sound got louder. That meant he was getting closer to whatever the dog had cornered.

Oh, shit, what if it's the breather? I don't have a weapon. Jim stopped to reason. *I don't know where I am in my own house. I must be on the second floor, Daisy sounds like she's far off.* As Jim continued on, he found a stairway, rough cut pieces of wood set in place. He tested each step by putting the weight down cautiously. Jim gripped the studs on each side of the passageway. It had some well-lit spots. Odd. How could it get illuminated?

Jim's heart pulsated wildly as fear raced through him. This seemed so strange. This house just wasn't typical. And he'd been trained to know better than let your concerns carry you away. He took a deep breath, "Daisy?"

"Woof, woof, woof," came her answer.

Jim pushed ahead. If she wasn't afraid why should he be. He should be because he knows how one human can impact another in a not so pleasant way. Daisy is expecting goodness all the days of her life. Jim knew not to expect some kind outcomes.

The path he followed continued down with no end in sight. Each step brought him closer to the pup. Soon he would know what Daisy knew. At least he hoped to. How many spiders lived in this human manufactured hallway. Jim couldn't even begin to count the webs. However, there were no webs around his body. That could only mean someone went through this hallway recently. They all seemed to be overhead and out of reach. He raised his chin. That's when he noticed what looked like skylights. Someone did some planning. He'd have to check to see if there were any leaks. Re-roofing was on his rehab list.

Jim went a little further and realized that he could be in the basement area, he'd gone down a long way. The steps stopped about the time he thought that.

Scuffing his feet told him he stood on dirt. This must be the first basement. I remember when Art and I were going through the turret room that someone living in that place seemed likely. Does the breather live there? Is it one person or more? They must be aware that I am getting close. They know me, every damn thing about me, and I know nada about them. Jim kept going, looking for any way out of this endless hallway to nowhere.

"Daisy?"

She came to him and whined then took off again. "I am coming." *Great now I am talking to a dog like she's a person.* When Jim managed to get to the spot Daisy waited, he could see she had dug at the wall enough to make a dent in the hard-packed surface.

His hand came up, and he rubbed the wall, looking for a handle to open the door. "Are you sure this is the place?"

Daisy whined.

"Okay." Jim searched more and finally found what he looked for. The handle opened the wall that moved like a barn door. It unlocked into another dugout room with a sink on one side and a dripping faucet, both barely visible in the dim light filtering from what Jim believed was the last skylight. The fear that someone might be waiting for him had his knees weak, "So, you have a private washroom of your own, whoever you are." Convinced now that someone else used these premises and confident that he wanted to find them and confront them inflamed his ire. He didn't notice that Daisy hunted on her own and had left him to ponder the area. How big is this darn property anyway? I wasn't going to gut this house, I wanted to leave the beauty of the time period in place. He had to tear it all down to find out what he and the records didn't know about this house and to find anything not up to permit. This little DIY project had to go.

Jim looked for the pup. Now what? "Daisy?"

"Woof."

Jim turned and looked hard at the far wall. A black drape hung there, and it sounded like Daisy barked from the other side of the curtain. Fear stabbed through him as he ventured forward, his hand grabbing the thick cloth. Like heavy drapery material, velvety to the touch, it didn't move smoothly. Jim leaned his head to peek into blackness. Why didn't he have a flashlight when he needed one. He pulled on the drape harder, and he could make room for his body to step behind. This would be uncomfortable going. Feeling his way around Jim took a step.

Breathing? Someone's breathing.

That fear thing happened to him again.

Daisy whined. Jim could hardly see the white fur, but she walked ahead of him back and forth like she attempted to get up on something high. Jim managed to cross that part of the dirt floor, and he bumped into what felt like a cot about shin level. He bent and ran his hand along the edge, his hand engulfing a strap and a freezing cold, heavy buckle. What the heck? Daisy climbed over Jim's feet and went the length of the cot. He had to be careful not to step on her. Jim wished that he smoked. He'd have matches or a lighter on him and could illuminate this dark dungeon. Jim worked his way down the cot and felt another buckle and the strap that went around a man's pant leg. Jim could feel the slacks material and the leather shoe and the laces. His hand searched up that shin bone. What the hell. "Shit, a body. Now there are dead people? Hello, can you hear me?"

No answer.

His eyes darted back and forth peering into the dense darkness. Wishing some illumination. He felt along the man's leg to the knee. What should he do? Frozen in place and not able to decide did not make Jim a happy man. He had enough information to get the police here and now. Jim turned to the drape and made his way back to the barn door.

Chapter Twenty-Eight

6:35 A.M. Sunday, October 22, 1995

Jim gulped down the fear that raced through his body and mind. He had felt the leg of a man. A corpse? There's a body in the house? My house! He had to get the police. No. He had to get a flashlight to see first for himself. The darkness in this area pressed in on him. Jim grabbed up Daisy and headed for the stairwell back up to his bedroom.

As he reached the opening into his bedroom, he noticed that the stairs continued on up, and that meant only one thing. Someone lived right now in that tower room and probably used this hallway to get from the outdoors to the upper chamber. Someone knows I'm on premises and aware of these passageways. And the eyes into my room. Who does that? He'd board them up as soon as possible and find this person and weed them out.

Where'd I put my flashlight? He looked around the spare room and spotted it just under his bed on the chair side. Jim reached for it and turned back to Daisy in time to see her wrap her body around the wall opening, and she took off. He went after her immediately shining the light as he went. Down and down he hurried, his clothing catching on the rough studs.

He slid his body back through the opening and went to the drape. Daisy whined, and he pulled the curtain aside to allow his body access. The flash beam flooded the darkness stabbing light in haloed dots here and there until Jim found the cot and ran the light up to the face.

Jim's mouth gaped. "Art?" Jim felt for the pulse, it seemed weak his wrist cold. He put his cheek by Art's mouth to feel the breath, but there didn't seem to be much. Art's pulse felt threadlike.

How could he get Art out of here? Jim flashed the beam all around looking for a way out. *There is no way. I can't carry him through that passageway. There has to be another way in here.* Jim turned and put his body into the hall again, rushing as fast as the tight area allowed, back upstairs, across his room to his phone. He called Walt.

Tracy came on the line and told him Walt hadn't come in yet this morning, but she'd have him call as soon as possible. Jim thanked her and called for an ambulance. How would they get him out? Instead of going back to Art he went to the basement and figured out which wall the passageway had to be on, and he began hitting the wall with a two by four, like a ram. The dirt wall held firm against the assault.

Jim realized he would not be able to reach Art that way. He ran back upstairs and out on the porch in time to see the ambulance pull up in his driveway. He motioned to the driver to follow him, and the man walked over to him.

"Come with me, I don't know how we are going to get him out right now."

The attendant narrowed his eyes but followed. Jim led him back to his bedroom, made sure he had the flashlight, and ducked into the passageway. The two made their way down to the basement area of the house, and Jim took him to Art.

The attendant checked Art's vitals in a speedy manner, turned on Jim and said, "What's going on here?"

"I don't know. I just found my friend a little while ago."

"You just found him? In here? How did he get in here?"

"That's just it, I don't know."

"Well, how'd you come to find him?"

Jim realized the rest of the morning promised to be insane. Could he tell this man that Daisy found him? That I heard someone breathing on the other side of the wall in my bedroom.

"Un huh!" He bent over and listened to Art's heart. "We need to get him to the hospital. Any idea how I can do that? How can I get my gurney in here?"

"I don't know, but doesn't it stand to reason that if he's here, he got in here somehow."

"And you own this place?"

"Yes,"

"And you don't know how he got in here?"

"That's right. Look Art's my friend. Can you help him or not?"

"Not without an exit plan." The attendant walked over to the dirt wall and moved along the side to the corner. "Help me!"

Jim went to him immediately.

"Let's see if we can move this." He gripped a handle and pushed down. It didn't move. He lifted, and it stayed put. "Well so much for that."

Jim ran his hand over the wall, and they worked their way to the other corner. Jim felt a handle very much like the one holding up the picture in his room. He twisted, just like he did with the one in his place. The wall slid, and Jim cast his light on the piles of dirt the police had dug up and left behind after they decided that no crime was committed. Well, maybe they are going to change their minds. "We can get him out. Come on, we'll bring the gurney down here this way." The two raced up through the basements into the dining room and out the front door. The attendant and his partner got busy unloading their gear and back they went, following Jim into the cellar and to Art.

"He's got a weak pulse."

Jim stepped back and let them ready Art for transportation. They counted numbers off together and picked up Art, moving him in one sweep. They strapped him down and soon headed out with him.

Jim's next job would be to get hold of Amanda and Melissa and get them to the hospital. At no time did Jim engage the thought that Art would not live. It just didn't pass his mind. As soon as they had Art on the gurney and out of the basement Jim went to the phone and began calling.

Amanda answered her cell and sounded tired. Jim told her Art was on his way to the hospital. It would be some time before he would be admitted, but to expect that Art would be and that he thought they should be there with him.

Amanda thanked him, and he heard her tell Melissa. "You're with Melissa?"

"Yes, I came to the station instead of going home. We've been together all night. Hopefully we can get sprung soon. Both of us could use a shower. "But listen, this is good news isn't it? Art's okay, right?"

"I think so. The paramedics took him to the hospital, and I'm going to go over there myself."

"Is he conscious?"

"It's better if you come to the hospital." He didn't want to tell them how bad it looked for Art. He chose to concentrate on the positive.

"He's not?" Amanda said.

"Concentrate on the positive right now. Will I see you there?"

"Yes."

Jim got off the phone and called the police. He told them of the visitor in his house, an unwanted visitor. That he wanted that person or persons evicted. The police officer Jim talked to left Jim with the impression someone would be right over. Jim hung out waiting for an officer to arrive. He decided, after a half hour went by, to go on to the hospital.

Chapter Twenty-Nine

An officer came to the door, shuffled into the room and said, "Walt says you can go". Amanda stretched and put her arms around Melissa's shoulders. "Keep in mind it won't do you any good to be angry at Walt. He would do anything to keep you safe, including letting you sit it out in a cell. So, remember, don't cross him again. You may not get a warning, you may get picked up and hauled to jail. Forgive him."

"I will never forgive Murphy. None of this would have happened if he would have kept his nose out of my business."

"Melissa," Amanda gave her a motherly look, "you know better than that."

"Yeah, but..."

"No buts. You need to fight the battles you can win."

"You sound just like my dad. He says things like that."

They were at the car and Amanda, with her arm still around her shoulders, squeezed once more before letting go, and they got into the vehicle. "We both need a shower, and look at our hair. I really don't want Art seeing me like this, but I don't care. I want to see him and that he's okay. Let's go see your dad."

Melissa nodded as she pulled the hair hanging in her face back, clearing her eyes. "I really want to go to the hospital first."

The engine caught and off they went. Pulling into the parking lot at the hospital, they raced into the lobby and asked for Arthur Franklin.

He had not been admitted, so they were told to check ER. They went there and found Doc Jim Wexford cooling his heels. He couldn't communicate any news. Art was off with the medical staff, and he had not been allowed to follow. They found chairs and sat waiting. Melissa watched the clock on the wall, its hand marching forward at a steady pace. An hour passed before someone came to talk to them.

Art would be admitted. He was under heavy sedation when he arrived. They tested and were waiting for the results to find out what was in his bloodstream. Hopefully, he'd be waking soon since no more sedation would be added. They would have to wait for the wearing off rate out for an unknown period.

"Will my dad be okay?"

"Time will tell," the Doctor said. And went on to say they would take good care of Art. The man in the white coat backed away, leaving them looking from one to the other.

"I guess we wait," Jim said, and he took them back to the lobby of the hospital and asked where Art would be taken. The clerk said she did not have that information yet.

"It's like he's here, but he isn't."

Walt came through the big glass doors and lumbered over to them. He smiled at Melissa who frowned at him. "I am glad you can be angry at me Mel. Glad I can see the expression on your face. So much better than wondering where you are and if you are okay. Or worst yet, viewing your cold dead body." He shook Jim's hand and Amanda's. "How is he?"

"We don't know. The doctor said Art was heavily sedated and they were testing to find out what's in his system."

"Walt, someone is living in the walls of my home. There's a secret passageway and, Oh, shit!" Jim stopped. "Daisy, she's caught in there." He turned to Melissa, "It's because of Daisy that I found Art. Daisy got onto the fact that someone was on the other side of the wall watching me while I slept. She dug at the wall, and I heard breathing when I went close, I found out how to open the wall and managed to follow the pup to Art, who was in the basement..." He turned to Walt, "by the mounds you guys dug up." Jim started backing away. "I've got to get her out of there. There's someone walking around that house and Daisy may not be safe."

"I'll send some guys," Walt said.

"I called, and they said they'd send someone, but they didn't come, and I came here to find out about Art."

"I'll get some people over there now."

"Thanks," he said looking directly at Walt and turned to Melissa and Amanda, "I'll be right back."

Jim trotted across the floor, pushed the glass door and ran across the parking lot to his car. He drove across town and out into the outskirts to his monster of a home. He left his car in the driveway and headed for the front door when a squad car pulled up and Murphy got out.

"Hi, Walt send you?"

"Don't know just who sent me, but I got a call to see the man at this address." They went into the house while

Jim explained the situation to Murphy and they decided to find Daisy and secure her and then begin the hunt for the mystery person. Jim took Murphy down to the basement the way they took Art out of the house. Daisy was not there. "Let me show you the passageway, and we will see if she's gone back up to the bedroom." The two men scooted through the tight route until they were at the opening. "See how the stairs continue up. I haven't taken that set yet, but I believe someone has been staying in the turret room. I think they've had run of this house for some time." Jim took Murphy into his bedroom, and they soon realized Daisy was not there.

"Daisy, come."

Jim walked to the bedroom door, "This has been shut, so I think she has to be in the passageway. Maybe she went up. Shall we?"

They reentered the tiny space and turned their attention to climbing up. The fit for the two larger men became tighter as they moved. Jim sucked in his gut and stood taller. The sound of their clothing brushing the siding filled the air. They managed to get to the end where the wall stopped their forward progress. "There has to be an opening." Jim felt all over the wall and finally found a hole that his hand could slip through. He felt for anything on the other side of the wall that might be a handle. Down his hand moved until Jim gripped a cold metal shaft. He pressed down, and the wall opened. Murphy slipped through, and then Jim followed.

"This is called the turret room. It at the top of the house and you can see from any of the windows all around the property."

Murphy walked over to the front window and looked down at the street. "Hey, isn't that Daisy?"

Jim came to the window and looked down. Daisy lie cuddled up by the trunk of the pine tree, sleeping. The sweetness of her moved Jim and he said, "We must have walked right by her. I didn't see her, did you?"

"No, but I wasn't looking down, and I wasn't looking for a dog."

"Let's get her, then we can figure out what to do next."

The two hurried down to the pine tree and picked up the little dog who showed her appreciation for being reunited with her people with pink tongue licks freely given.

Murphy began the search from top to bottom as Jim waited on the front porch holding Miss Daisy in his lap, stroking her beautiful fur. When Murphy finished, he came to stand by Jim and explained how he'd searched and found nothing that would prove someone had been there.

"What about the picture with the cut-out eyes and the hole in the wall on the other side of that hallway to the turret room. What about the breathing. What about Daisy digging at the wall. Daisy knows there was someone there."

"I don't think that's going to hold up in a court of law," Murphy said.

"Well, do you think that the person will come back?"

"I can't really say anything about that."

"This is a fine kettle of fish, I can't get any help from the police?"

"I can't arrest the thin air. Who do you suggest I cuff?"

Chapter Thirty

9:12 A.M. Sunday, October, 22, 1995

From Jim Wexford's home one could follow the movement of the vehicles that came and went down the two-lane country road, hear the lowing of the cattle in the nearby pasture and see, if you looked carefully, at the baby goats frolicking and climbing over each other in the neighbor's lot to the east. Other than that activity, the two men stood on the old wooden porch with heavy hearts. A mystery needed solving.

Jim, holding Daisy with his arm under her chest and ribcage, stared into the walnut orchard across the street, following the neat rows until they merged. Daisy turned her head and followed both men as they talked.

Shadows fell across the porch, chilling the area. Birds sang songs all around, and nothing about this place suggested adverse events such as Jim worried about.

"Given that you and I were just in the... let's call it the squatters quarters, and no one was there, that means the person or persons in question must have other hiding places here on the property," Murphy said, as his hand glided over Daisy's head and neck.

It seemed to Jim that Murphy talked more to the dog than to him.

"I would agree." Jim smiled at Daisy, who licked his thumb. "She is cute, hard not to love, and she is a hero."

"Yeah. She is that." Murphy looked up at the pine growing beside the walk following it to the tip and to the turret windows.

Jim noticed his gaze. "I'm not making this up. If it weren't for this dog, I would not have found Art. Because someone made a walkway from the cellar to the turret room. That person is still around. And, it's just plain creepy to think someone's going to be watching me sleep tonight."

"I've got to get back in there, and I am going to call in backup. Since we don't know who at this point, we don't know how dangerous this person, or persons are. I have to err on the side of safety."

"Call in the National Guard, I don't care. Just find and get them out. It's like they've leeched onto my home. They are sucking me dry while they have the run of the place. It's disturbing having someone looking through a picture at you while you sleep. I don't know if I'll be able to sleep in that room. At least until I know they are gone."

Murphy nodded. The two took steps apart as though they agreed to part. "I'll get going on this. You're headed back to the hospital?"

"Yes, I'll be there as long as needed. You can reach me there with good news I hope. Oh, I can't take her."

Jim handed Daisy to Murphy who said, "I'll take care of her. Her backyard cage would be the best place for her. I'll make sure there's water and food for her, and you can check on her later, is that okay?"

"You're going to take her to Art's?"

"Yes, that okay?"

"Great." Jim turned away, nodded and waved his hand. "Later." He opened the car door and headed back to the hospital.

The parking lot had space after space filled, Jim found one at the outer edge. He ran across the lot to the sidewalk and quickly stepped along to the glass doors and went inside. He strolled briskly to the desk and signed in and asked for Art's room number. His head spun toward the elevators, and he thanked the clerk volunteer.

To the elevator and the up button. Jim looked to see where the lift currently moved. Coming down, great.

He stepped inside and that feeling of fear and claustrophobia creeped into him like a cloud and he wondered, *will this thing get me where I want to go, or will it fail to open when it does.* He looked up at the hatch, a small dark square in a heavily paneled cell. His foot moved over a floral print that seemed old. Didn't sway his thoughts of; *will I end up crawling out of this damned elevator to get free? I hate elevators.* The elevator started up, and he had that weightless sense like he needed to move his feet to catch his balance. In a second he'd reached the third floor, and the elevator rocked in place. He stared at the door. It seemed to stare back until a settling sound like a soft clunk happened just before the suction broke its seal and fresh air, well, hospital circulated air met him, and he felt relieved to be stepping into the hall. Truth be known he didn't like hospitals.

Art's room waited to the left of where he stood. He moved that direction and went around a corner and into the room. Amanda and Melissa were standing beside his bed, and Art met Jim with the biggest widest closed-mouth grin he could make. His eyes sparkled, and Jim realized they were tears. Art barely held it all back, and that smile told Jim so much about what swam around inside Art's head.

The face seemed scrubbed, a light stubble barely beginning, the hair combed back in a way Art never did his hair. Jim tipped his head to get his mind around what he saw. Two women were clasping hands together, Amanda's other hand rested on a light beige blanket covering Art's leg.

"Well, it's good to see him awake," Walt said.

Startled, Jim turned and saw Walt sitting in a chair. "Can you take these two down for some breakfast and let me have a talk with Art?"

"Sure."

Amanda and Melissa protested but followed Jim's direction when he took Melissa's elbow. "I don't know when you ate last, and I wonder if you even know?"

"What happened?" Walt said as soon as they were out of the room and their footsteps receded into silence.

"I can't remember anything. My head's swimming. I remember hearing a dripping sound off to my right, I think. Someone, a woman I think would stand beside me and I fell off to sleep. Drugged me. That's all I can think of."

"Art?"

"Yeah?"

Walt came close on the open side of the bed and leaned over. "Do you remember the tape recording of the bird that you had?"

Art narrowed his eyes, shook his head.

"You came to the station and played a tape for me, and we thought it might be some drama club play or something like that. Remember?"

The expression on Art's face said that he had no idea what Walt was talking about.

174

Walt shuffled closer to the bed. "Do you remember the names on that tape?"

"I can't remember anything about a tape, Walt, my head is swimming and I can't keep focused on any one thing right now. It's hard to even finish a sentence. I want to nod off."

"Okay, well, I've got a body, and I think that tape might be a clue in breaking the case. I think this guy is the same one mentioned on that tape. I really need you to remember. Tell me where that tape is. I need to hear it again. You going to be okay?"

"I think so."

"What did the doc say?"

"I don't remember, I'll find out later."

"Let me know. And try to remember. You said something about a dead bird. You found it at Jim's house along with the tape."

"Did you ask Jim?"

"Yeah, but he said you had the tape. You took it to Yvonne's and then to me, and that is all he knows. He buried the bird. I had him dig it up, and I have it now in the freezer."

"I didn't give the tape to you?"

"No, we listened to it and decided it was some play or whatever."

Art nodded, and his mustache tweaked. "I wish I could help, but I am out of it man, out of it. Do you know what they pumped into me?"

"Who, the doc?"

"No, whoever was drugging me."

Walt shook his head, "Not a clue."

Chapter Thirty-One

10:20 A.M. Sunday, October, 22, 1995

Flat gray walls seemed to float around to a window that opened out to a courtyard filled with trees that Art could see from his hospital bed. The leaves were turning. That meant it was fall. Art's hand rubbed over the ribbed blanket over his legs, sensing its softness. He couldn't settle on the year, and for some reason it didn't matter a whole hell of a lot that the leaves were changing. He looked away to the framed picture of a girl swinging a full skirt in a field of poppies. Pleasant enough. Behind her a river ambled and he fixed on it.

Rio? Rio? Why do I think about that? What is it? A river? A name? Why am I thinking about that? It won't go away. Rio what? What can it mean? Art scratched behind his ear. The fog shrouding his mind right now made clear thinking impossible. Dreams filled his mind with shrouded forms floating in and out? Dreams filled spaces and voids. Nothing jelled and as hard as he tried to worry, which as everyone knew was his natural state, he could not. Art couldn't even care very long about the odd word, 'Rio' that kept coming to him. Somewhere in the depths of his mind he knew he should.

The doc came into his room, and he turned at the sound of her foot fall. She appeared to float as she came closer, and she spoke softly. Art liked the sound of her voice. Her hair reminded him of Melissa's, short and sassy, but brown, not his girls coppery red. *His girl's.* A smile plumped his cheeks.

The doc smiled in return and nodded. "We've narrowed down the drugs we found in your system. You had quite a cocktail. Cocaine, heroin, clonazepam, and gabapentin. None of them were prescribed for you. We don't know how they got into your system." Her lips pouted together to make emphases of her words. "You could have died. Probably would have if you didn't get in here when you did."

She unloaded all this on him as though he could register it and process the information. He couldn't. Instead, it sailed fleetingly over his head, leaving him struggling to form questions.

Someone tried to kill me?

She picked up his chart intent on the information.

Why? Why would anyone want to do this to me? All I've ever done is help people.

A phone rang somewhere.

Should I answer it?

"What are you looking for?" she asked.

"The phone."

"Oh, don't worry. Someone will answer it."

He tried to smile and then the thought settled. *I became a policeman to help my community. I'm a policeman!* That was a bit of a surprise, but then again it felt right.

The doc continued to talk and inform him as though Art was able to understand. Instead, the residual of the drugs allowed his mind to do its thing, and that was to wander from one subject to the next unfiltered.

"You'll get back to normal in short time. I'd like to keep you here until you are steadier. Tomorrow you can go home if you keep progressing as you are now. Rest today, and I'll see you tomorrow."

Art listened to her but couldn't get his mind to focus on anything other than who would do this to him. *And, what did happen? Everything's just fuzzy.* "How did I get here?"

The doc raised her eyebrows, "The paramedics brought you in. You were a mess. We had a time figuring out what all was going on."

Art half smiled at her. His brain wouldn't function no matter how hard he tried. All he wanted to do was shut his eyes. "When will I be awake?"

"Fully, that may take some time. We've reversed the drugs in your system with a cocktail of our own, but your system will need to work things out at its own pace. Rest today and let's see how you are in the morning." The doc nodded, held the clipboard to her chest and backed out of his room.

His eyes were shut before she stepped over the threshold. He couldn't even fathom when tomorrow was.

Melissa, she was here with Amanda. They held hands. He smiled. *Walt came, and so did Jim. Everything is okay at home.* His mind settled a bit. As he slipped off, "*Rio*" circled.

A figure slithered into his room, came to his bedside, and leaned to his ear. "Art Franklin, where is the tape?"

"Hum…" Art said.

Across town, at the Franklin residence, Melissa opened the door and three officers marched into the foyer. Melissa smiled at them, "My dad's going to be okay. Thanks for coming by."

She expected them to say something along the lines of how glad they were to hear that, but they didn't.

"We are here to search the place. Walt says he hopes he doesn't need a warrant."

"What!" Melissa's face expressed every shocked expression. "Now?"

"Yes, Miss Franklin, now."

Her shoulders slumped, she and Amanda wanted a cup of cocoa, a hot shower, and a nap. That's all they talked about on the ride home from the hospital. "What are you looking for?" She squinted her eyes, partly from exhaustion and somewhat because she wondered if Walt was jerking her around again. If he was, it didn't sit well with her at this moment.

The tea kettle whistled and stopped almost as soon as it began. Amanda must have taken it off the stove. That means the cocoa will be ready. Not enough for them. Well, we could make more. "You're kidding, right?"

"No. Afraid not."

"Any point asking what you are looking for?"

"A tape that has a message Walt wants now."

She thought of her dad's office and wondered about the door. *Is it open or locked? If its locked the key will be in my dad's pants pocket. Crap, what…. am I thinking? That stupid jerk Murphy kicked it in.* "I guess you can start in there." She pointed toward the office and headed for the kitchen. "Let me know when you find it and when you leave."

"Yes, ma'am."

Amanda poked at her marshmallow, Melissa was blowing on her mug's contents when the cops strolled into the kitchen.

"Find anything?" Melissa gazed toward them with malice on her face.

"We are going upstairs; would you like to accompany us, Miss Franklin?" The taller officer said.

Melissa's fingers tightened around the mug, "Why, so I know which one of you trashed what?"

"No, just letting you know we have finished with the office, the living room, and the foyer. We will go through the kitchen after we do the upstairs."

"You want us out?" Amanda said, looking at the cop that spoke.

He shook his head, the expression on his face happy. "Yeah, something like that."

"Come on honey lets go out by the pool." They took their steaming mugs and gave the men sour looks, taking Daisy with them they let the screen door slam.

"Boy, what else could happen? My eyes are burning. Like I've been up too long."

"They are probably dry. As soon as the cops leave, I'll go too, and you can get your shower and get some sleep. You will feel a whole lot better."

"I don't think I want this second cup of cocoa." Melissa yawned. "I feel like calling Walt and asking him to call them off and let us get back to normal."

"It's worth a try. I think Walt would understand, considering all that's been happening."

One of the cops came out to the poolside where they sat.

"Pardon me, Miss Melissa, your dad's car is here. Where do you want it?"

"What do you mean it's here?"

"The tow truck needs to unload it, and they want to know what you want to do with it."

"Where are they?"

"Out front."

Melissa set her mug on the edge of the Adirondack chair's arm and headed for the side gate and the front of the house. When she got there a heavy-set man with black suspenders over a white T-shirt was working at unhooking the car. "Where do you want it?"

"Can you put it in the garage?"

"Sure."

When the car sat in its spot and the garage door remained open, he offered the clipboard to Melissa to sign her name. She did, and he got into his truck and drove off.

The cops were all over the car the minute that the truck left and Melissa turned to go back to Amanda by the pool.

"Knock yourselves out." She said into the air.

Melissa went back to Amanda. She sat down again. "I'm so tired, I don't think I can handle one more thing today," she said through a yawn.

"Me too. That's part of the reason I didn't follow you out front. I knew there wasn't anything I could do and you could handle it just fine," Amanda said and yawned. "My eyes are watering. I know I've said it a thousand times already, but I am so glad we found Art and he's in the hospital where he is safe."

"Me too."

Chapter Thirty-Two

10: 25 A.M. Sunday, October 22, 1995

Jim walked through the front door of his home only to be met by an officer. "Sir, this is an ongoing investigation, and we need you to leave."

His shoulders dropped, from fatigue, from so many things. He could go back to the Franklin's, guessed he would do that. "Have you found anyone?"

"Not able to say at this point." The officer barred his way.

"Can I get some clothes?"

"Not at the moment."

Jim nodded and left. *Lousy stuff at this house just goes on and on.* He drove back to the Franklin's and saw the cop cars out front. He hesitated, not knowing what he should do. He could get a hotel or motel room. Jim watched the cops going through Art's car, and one of them noticed him. He walked over to Jim, and Jim figured he'd get run off here too. The officer leaned in, and Jim let the passenger side window all the way down. His arms rested on the open window ledge, and he placed his face in the open window. "Miss Franklin and Amanda are out back by the pool. We are almost finished here."

Jim nodded and rolled up the window, turned off the car and walked to the girls. They held mugs and had the same exhausted expression he figured he offered. "Hi." He took a chair. "I've been kicked out of my place again. Can I stay here?"

Amanda looked at Melissa. As she did, Jim gazed her way too.

"Sure, don't know how the house is going to be once they are out of here, but sure. The more the merrier. Isn't that the saying?" She held up her mug. "Want some cocoa?"

Jim shook his head. "All I want is a shower and my own bed. Oh, no I don't. Not until they find that person that's been watching me."

Amanda shot a startled eye his way, "What?"

"Someone cut some eyes out of a painting and a hole in the wall behind so their face would fit and they watched me while I was in my bedroom. They also are the ones responsible for Art being in my basement. I think."

Melissa sat forward. "Someone in your house put my Dad in the basement and kept him there?"

Jim nodded. "That's what I think."

"You don't know this person?"

"No."

She sat even more forward, "The cops are going through your place looking for this person now?"

Jim nodded.

"Boy, Walt's got to be royally pissed."

"Why?"

Melissa grinned. "He's an old teddy bear and likes to work with my dad to figured things out. He's got more than one front. He's got the hospital, to keep dad safe, this house for the tape, your house for some person or persons…"

"And, he's got you."

"Me?"

"Oh yeah, he's really concerned you might be a target. He talked with me about it that night at the station when I called him. I think that is why he let us out of the cell and into that room," Amanda said.

"Well, I am okay. And there are plenty of people around me. You think it's not over? Whatever is going on?"

"I don't think it's over, not until we understand what has happened. Why take your dad and drug him? What is the reason?"

"Yeah, that's just crazy. What could my dad have done to make someone do that? He could have died."

Amanda reached over and patted her arm, "Thank God he didn't."

"How did you find him?" Melissa looked up expectantly.

"I didn't. Daisy found your Dad."

Melissa's mouth gaped. "Daisy?"

"You mentioned a tape. The cops are looking for a tape?"

"Yeah, I don't know anything about it." Jim sat deeper and gazed off across the river.

Amanda picked up on his change, "Jim, you know about this tape?"

His head nodded, "I might."

"Do you know where it is?" Melissa asked.

"Your dad had it last. We found it in the turret room at my house along with the dead bird."

184

"That's why the police were going over this place, for that tape."

Yeah, I think so," Jim said.

"Dead bird? "Amanda asked.

"Yeah, an African grey parrot. I looked it up in the bird book, and it's thought of as the most intelligent and talkative of the parrots," Jim said.

"What happened to it?"

"I buried it."

"Oh," Melissa said.

"But that's not the end of the story. It seems, I gleaned from what little the police let out, that the bird might be mixed up with that body found in the river."

"The one I thought was my Dad?"

"Yeah, Walt must have figured it out too because he came over and had me dig the bird up. He's got it now in a freezer."

"What's he going to do with a dead bird?"

"I don't know."

Melissa laughed, "He probably plans to use it as a witness."

"A witness to what, the person watching me sleep?"

"How did you figure that out?"

"Daisy, she kept digging at the wall, and I came over to see what she was doing. I heard some breathing, and then I could actually hear some movement behind the wall where I stood. Someone was there. When I got the wall to open Daisy scooted into the passageway and took off, and she went down a very narrow winding odd staircase to the basement and found your dad. I followed of course, and the rest is history."

Melissa grabbed her arms and stroked them. "That's just too weird."

Amanda yawned again and stretched, almost spilling her cocoa. "You've come up with some doozies over the years Jim, but this one's the best." She stood. "I've got to get some sleep, and I want to see Walt as soon as I can. I also want to get back to the hospital. What are you two going to do?"

"Jim, I am headed for a shower and a nap, then I'm going back to the hospital. You can give me a ride if you don't mind," Melissa said.

"That works for me. I need a shower, and I want to get back to Art. I'd also like a word with Walt." Jim stood. "I think we are all on the same page. What are we waiting for?"

"Those guys. As soon as they leave, we can do our thing."

"Oh yeah. I forgot about them."

Jim stood, "I'll go find out. I'll be back."

Amanda reached over and took Melissa's hand and squeezed it. "We will get through this, and we will be okay."

Jim came back and said the cops were leaving and they didn't find the tape.

"Guess we are going to have to wait for Art to tell us what the tape is all about."

"I guess."

Amanda rose and placed her hand on Jim's arm. "I'll see you two at the hospital in three hours. Does that sound okay?"

"Yeah."

"Works for me."

Chapter Thirty-Three

10:40 A.M. Sunday, October 22, 1995

Amanda left Jim and Melissa and started home, but steered her car to the police station instead. She walked to Walt's office door and draped herself against the jamb. Walt held his forehead in the palms his hands, elbows on the desktop and seemed to be studying the desk mat.

"You sleeping?" She said.

"No," Walt said and looked up. "Anything new?"

"I was on my way home to get a shower and some sleep, then we are going back to the hospital in three hours. Something made me come here. Do you have any news?"

He looked up. The light in the room made his lines and wrinkles stand out. The bags under his eyes were deep purple and dusty blue. "Melissa home?"

"Yeah." Amanda heaved her body off the jamb and over to the chair. She sighed as she sat. "Jim is with her.

Guess your guys are over at his house and they won't let him in there."

Walt parted his lips and licked the bottom one. "Coffee?"

"No, thanks."

Walt jerked up, held his hands out expressively and said, "Here it is, I have nothing but questions. Who was the body in the river? It's got a tattoo that says "Rio" on his chest, and one bullet went through the 'O' as though planned. He's on ice. I've got a dead bird. It's on ice." Walt's hands swung out and around. "I've got an old partner who might as well be on ice. You can't ask him a question and get an answer. He's all over the place, and then he just goes to sleep. They say he's going to be that way for a while. I've got Melissa who could be a target and won't assist in her wellbeing. I've got someone running around in the walls of an old turn-of-the-century house who may or, may not be a killer and to top it all off a missing tape that may or may not have anything to do with the "Rio thing". The hands continued to fly through the air. Walt fixed his whole attention on Amanda's eyes. "Art might hold the key to this whole mess, but he can't tell me, or remember where he put the tape."

"Sounds to me like you could use some sleep too."

Slowly his lids dropped and closed for a bit then lifted as though a ton weighed them down. "Sleep, what's that?"

Her grin didn't help.

"I'd like to go home. I probably wouldn't sleep, and I'd just get up and come back down here." He looked down at the mat, and the room quieted until he heard their breathing. He sighed. "Art would tell me to start at the beginning again. That's what he always did when things didn't work out, he'd go back and pull another string. The only thing is, I don't know where there's another string to pull. Everything's a mess. You sure Melissa's okay?"

"She's worn out Walt. That cell idea of yours turned out to be hard on her. She just wanted to find her dad, and she believed no one wanted to find him but her."

"I know." He heaved a sigh.

They both turned toward the door as Yvonne smacked her cane down with each step and tapped her way into the room. Neat and well-groomed, she contrasted the two of them.

"You two look like you went a couple of rounds with the latest heavyweight." She looked from one to the other. "And lost! What in God's green earth is going on?"

Amanda smiled a crooked pulling of her lips, "I feel like that. How are you, Yvonne?"

"I'm great. What about Art?"

Walt sat back in his rolling chair as though he'd been smacked again and Amanda studied her shoes.

"We don't know pretty much everything at this point."

"Has he been found?"

"Yes. You hadn't heard?"

A sour expression crossed her face. "No. I'm out of the loop as usual, except when I can be of value to this department."

Walt ran his hand over his chin and to his loosened tie. "He's in the hospital. He was drugged, and he's not awake yet. I'd love to talk with him and I will as soon as he's lucid. The doc says maybe tomorrow."

"What kind of drugs?"

"Walt, do you know? "Amanda asked.

"Yes, a cocktail that could have killed him. It would have if he weren't found. It's got me. What it's all about? Why drug him? The only thing I can come up with is that the perpetrator is after his daughter and they were luring

189

Melissa to them. I don't know how or when, but that's the only thing that makes any sense to me."

"Huh! For what purpose?" Yvonne said.

Walt pointed to a chair by the back wall, "Let me get that chair for you." He made his way, and Yvonne moved to the left to allow him to place the chair next to Amanda's.

"Thanks."

Slouching back behind his desk Walt spoke in a husky voice, "I don't know." Walt shrugged his shoulders, "All I know is that Art came in here with a tape. We listened to it and decided that it meant nothing. Now I have a dead body with a strange name tattooed on his chest. A bullet hole shot through it, and the body has red hair. I might add, from what I can remember from hearing on that tape, I am convinced it plays a part in all this. I've got to find that tape."

"What significance does the red hair have?" Yvonne asked.

"It got Melissa's interest. It very well could have been the carrot that lured her to the person or persons perpetrating this little act of evil."

Amanda sat forward, "She thought it was her dad and she took off for the river. Separating her from us, her protectors."

"Exactly, that's why I think she's the target," Walt said.

"Who?" Yvonne said, narrowing her eyes.

"Yes, who would do this? What's the motive?" Walt said.

"Art came into my office about ten days ago and wanted to play that tape."

Walt brightened, "You heard it?"

Yvonne shook her head, and the salt and pepper hair didn't even move. "I gave him my player, and he went into the inner office. He listened to it alone and then left. I didn't hear anything."

"Well, that's a big help." Walt shoved back from his desk. "That's the way this whole case goes, a little string to pull and it disappears like smoke in the wind." His hand, fingers together, opened as though to let something free.

Yvonne cleared her throat. "Well I could do a little poking around. Off the books. The McNamare's might be a good place to check."

"The Mister has been out fishing this week. Seems he enjoys the pastime."

"And the Mrs.?"

"I haven't any information about her." Walt stood up and walked to the counter located behind his desk and picked up a manila folder. "All the information on the couple is in here. You can look it over if you want."

Yvonne's hand lifted outstretched and waiting. "I want."

Walt handed the file to her, but before he gave it up he said, "Have Tracy make a copy for you. This file stays with me. I don't think anything's going to turn up."

Yvonne nodded and opened the file. She read a few pages and closed the folder. "This pretty much mirrors what I have on file. I would bet that these two could very well be at the bottom of this mess with Art. They probably believe that the loss of their grandson is a direct result of Art's actions. They might want revenge."

"I am not so sure," Amanda weighed in. "They know after the failed attempt on Art's life a few weeks ago that the police will be looking their way if anything happens to Art or Melissa."

"But crazies don't think clearly. And crazies do what they want when they want without care or concern for their future. They often think they have no worries because their actions are justified," Yvonne said.

Walt looked from Yvonne to Amanda. "You're the professional on head jobs, what do you think?"

Amanda turned from Walt to Yvonne. "Go for it girl."

Chapter Thirty-Four

11:15 A.M. Sunday, October 22, 1995

Yvonne shoved her cane into the back seat of her sedan and settled herself in the front seat. The P.I. in her adjusted her sunglasses and turned the car on. Yvonne rotated her neck to see behind and grimaced from the discomfort that action caused. Her lips tightened as she turned back around, reached for the seatbelt and pulled it around and clipped it into the socket. As Yvonne did that a scene flashed before her eyes, cold shivers raced over her, her hand, almost to the ignition halted as she studied the mystical event.

She could not be in two placed at once. Yvonne fumbled in her purse and pulled out her phone. "Lessie, I need you to get over to the hospital and cover Art." She listened to Lessie's surprised response and answered her, "Yes, Art Franklin." She talked to Lessie some more and explained. "I don't know, just a feeling. I doubt the police are covering him, he's out of the office on leave. Walt may not have thought it important since he's fixated on Melissa's safety. But I just got one of my instincts, and it's a gut one. I'm busy, and you are the best one for this detail. So, get your butt over there now and stay until I tell you different."

That out of the way, she turned back to the matter at hand. She drove with a purpose. Her plan, not entirely formed yet, stirred her mind to action and she figured she would wing it. Something she could claim to be good at. She stopped her car around the corner from the McNamare place and grabbed some business cards from the box in the door well. She removed about ten and shoved them into her pants pocket.

Finally, she left the interior of the car, opened the back door, retrieved her cane, locked the car and gathered all the visual information about the neighborhood that she could. Quiet, well-kept yards, newer cars parked around. No sign of young children, toys left out, or basketball setups. This would be an older neighborhood. People probably lived here all their lives and raised their children here. An excellent place to get information.

She steadied herself, making sure her right foot waited for her to tell it to move. Yvonne leaned on the cane and the right foot lifted, she wobbled slightly as she placed her balance over the right leg and brought the left foot up and made the second step. Since breaking her back at the police department as a cop twelve years ago, walking had become a sporting event. She never knew if she would finish her planned path of execution or not. It pretty much pissed her off and kept her in that state most of the time. She had Lessie do many of the active tasks. Which also pissed her off, well, she guessed just about anything could piss her off, including Art Franklin. *So, why in hell am I doing this for him? Because I'm such a nice person.* "Right!"

Her thoughts kept pace with the tapping of her cane as she went up the walk to the corner house, the house that was, if her eyes told her accurately, three houses away from the McNamare home. She'd rattle a few cages on her way to the target—Emily McNamare. A smile broke her steely face. Let the fun begin.

"Hello! I am Grace Kelly, a real estate investor and I wanted to get some information about this neighborhood. I have a buyer interested in a home here, and he wanted to know about the crime in the area?"

The woman on the other side of the screen door unlatched the screen, and her lovely hand escaped the confines of the wood and screen to take the card Yvonne extended. Yvonne noticed the soft pink nail polish that glowed from her fingertips.

"My husband and I have been in the area for forty years. This is a nice quiet neighborhood." She slipped past the screen door and pointed to some chairs to the left of them. "It's been a long time since anyone's been interested in our little area. I don't think any of the houses are for sale. No one leaves." She pulled one of the wicker chairs for Yvonne. "Grace, is that what you said your name was?" She looked at the business card.

"Yes." Yvonne smiled as she sat and found a place for the cane to rest. "I wondered. There don't seem to be any signs on the lawns anywhere."

"I don't think there will be any. We had a block party about a month ago, and no one said anything about moving."

"You've been here forty years; did you raise your children here? How did you like the schools?"

The woman's white blouse's collar turned crisply over her bright blue V neck sweater. Yvonne thought it a bit too warm for such attire but didn't let on. "Oh, my name's Lynndee Meyers. It's nice to meet you, Grace." She extended her hand to Yvonne.

"Nice to meet you too. "So, how many children did you have, Lynndee?"

"We, Warren and I, had two boys and one girl. They are all married and moved away. They've said how they would like to live here, but, there are no places available."

"You like to knit? Did you make your sweater?"

Her pink tipped fingers lovingly caressed the knit by her tummy. "Thank you for noticing. Yes, I love to knit."

"I knit too, made an afghan for a Christmas present."

"Oh, I do that too. What pattern did you use?"

Shit, why did I have to say I could knit. "Don't think I can say right off. It had some wavy rows, really pretty." Yvonne hoped that would be enough to sail her home-grown girl story past this woman.

"How big did you make it?"

Great, how big. I don't know, what shall I say. "It was for a man. He'd been hurt, and it covered his legs. He'd been in a shooting, and I felt sorry for him."

"Oh, wow. That's awful. Sounds like what happened to my neighbor, Emily and her grandson Ray."

"Really?"

"Yeah! The boy was no good." Lynndee sought out Yvonne's eyes. "If you know what I mean. That one was always in trouble and his grandmother, Emily, she's my friend, always told me he was going to be the death of her. And then, poof, one day, the boy is gone. Shot!"

Yvonne allowed an expression of surprise to cover her face. "No!"

"Yes." She nodded. "Killed by one of Lodi's detectives on the courthouse steps in Stockton.

"Oh, my, that must have been awful for your friend. How did she take it?"

196

"That's funny. Now that you ask, Emily hasn't said word one about it. You'd think she would. But not to me."

'Well, she probably has the help of family. Some people grieve privately."

"Yeah, but her husband," Lynndee moved closer, her eyes narrowed, "He's always gone. Fishing. He pulls that boat out and off he goes, and I think Emily's a fishing widow. I don't think he supports her very much. Emotionally I mean. I got the feeling he didn't back her up in raising that boy."

"She raised the boy?"

"Yeah, Emily's son and his wife died in a car crash when the boy was a baby. I think Emily was mom and dad to the boy." Lynndee nodded.

"She's been a stay at home mom, or grandmom?"

"Yeah, I'd say that."

Yvonne smiled at the woman. "Well, I thank you so much for helping me. If you are interested in selling, or you know someone who is, please keep me in mind." She pointed to the card Lynndee held, gathered her cane and tapped her way next door. No one answered the door, so she tucked the card into the screen door space, wiggling it to make sure it would not slip out.

Yvonne noticed Lynndee followed her progress as she made her way to Emily McNamare's door and waited for her to answer her doorbell. "Hi, I am Grace Kelly. I'm a real estate investor, and I have a buyer interested in a home in this neighborhood. Can you tell me something about the schools and the area? Have you been here long?" Emily looked like a sweet enough woman in her sixties. Her white hair lay neatly over her head and waved on the sides, softening the frame around her face. She had a ready smile and twinkling eyes. Yvonne thought she might like this woman. She didn't seem like the kind to kill, or drug someone to get even.

"I doubt I can be of any help. I don't think anyone wants to sell. We've all lived together for so long we just might finish our lives out together. As far as the schools are concerned, they are good. It's been a while since I had any kids in school, but I guess you could find out about the schools somehow."

This woman's not our scum bag. I'd bet my life on that. "So, you feel it's a safe place to bring up children?"

"Oh, my yes." She started closing the door. "I'm sorry but I've got something in the oven, and I need to get back to my stove."

"Thank you," Yvonne said and turned away. *If it's not the McNamare's going after Art now, who is?*

Chapter Thirty-Five

11:30A.M. Sunday, October 22, 1995

Lessie put the phone down, turned off the computer, grabbed a giant purple sling with two strap handles that she then deftly slung over her shoulder. Her hand sank in deep as she fished out her keys and locked Tango Investigation's office door. Off she trotted for the parking lot and her older white sedan, the one she would never be able to part with. It started right up, and she drove over to the Lodi Memorial Hospital, marched into the foyer and met up with two sets of people she knew. They talked a few moments and then she headed for the sign-in desk, identifying herself and asking for Art Franklin's room number.

Soon the elevator dropped to a soft stop, and the door eased opened. Lessie stepped out onto the quiet carpet and followed the hall to the room. Yvonne was right, no one sat out front guarding Art. She walked into Art's hospital room and saw his mouth gaping open, golden red stubble crowding his chin and jawline. The man looked years older than she remembered. Tears seeped from the edges of his closed eyes. Something didn't seem right to Lessie, but she didn't know what. He breathed, that seemed clear. Her hand went under his nose to check and the hot breath puffed over the back of her hand. Lessie decided to sit off to the side, out of the way, in a metal chair she spotted by the drape. This would be a long stake-out, she resolved. The man would not be having many visitors until he could communicate and that didn't look like anytime soon.

Lessie moved over to the chair and repositioned it so that the drape hid her from anyone entering the room. She dropped her bag on the floor and cringed. She hated putting her purse on the floor, not knowing what crud would be on the bottom when she picked it back up, but there was no other place, and Lessie didn't want to have to think about its safety as she watched Art. The floor it would have to be. Her foot shoved it under her chair. Gripping the fabric, she began pulling the drape to hide her body. It slipped along silently settling just above her knees as she sat. Lessie had a limited view of Art's head from the edge of the curtain. She shut her eyes allowing her acute hearing to take over the surveillance. Her ears soon caught the usual sounds of the hospital. She'd spent a load of time here with different people. It felt like a second home, and she thought, one of the best places in town to get a good meal. The doctors knew her by sight and name. Because of that, she wanted to be incognito, not wanting to answer questions about why she was here. She liked Art, but keeping him safe didn't need to be a public affair.

After ten minutes where she'd shut her eyes and tuned her listening skills outward, she heard foot shuffling and figured it to be a nurse coming to check on Art. One eye opened, and she quickly realized this was not a nurse or an orderly with health care on their minds. Oh, they wore scrubs, but that was as far as it went. What scheme did this person have? *It's a woman, that much I know.* Lessie's eyes were on her now. Curiosity peaked.

She sat cold stone still, limited her breathing and became as invisible as possible. The woman came close and leaned over Art. Lessie tried to see the person's hands but the slice of drape kept them hidden. *Those hands, what were they doing?* One was completely out of view. Then the other came into view as it rested over Art's chest. Seemed innocent enough, but not. Lessie kept surveillance. The woman spoke, but Lessie didn't get it all. *It sounded like "Art…. Ape."*

Louder idiot, I can't hear you. The woman stayed a few seconds longer and backed away. Art didn't move a muscle, nor did he answer her question. Lessie thought about her next move. *If I leave this spot, this person will know that I know they were in this room and talking with Art. If I don't go after her, I won't know who she is or be able to ID her in the future. That's important!* Lightning speed moved Lessie off the chair and to the doorway. The hall was filled with people, many looking just like the woman who just left Art. She looked both directions. Some had their heads together talking. The woman wouldn't be one of them. She'd be alone moving away. There were several. Lessie didn't get an idea of the woman's height, great. Yvonne would be all over that. *The woman's gone in a sea of people.* Lessie turned and checked Art. He hadn't changed or moved. Nothing more she could do.

Lessie went back to her seat. She shrugged off the near miss and waited for the next one. When it happened,

Lessie would be ready. This time she'd find out what the woman wanted.

At three Jim and Amanda with Melissa came into the room. They whispered as they surrounded the bed. Lessie went out of her cubby hole and let them know she was there.

"Lessie," Melissa said. "Have you been here long?"

"Yeah. Yvonne put me on duty. Figured the department probably didn't have Art covered, so here I am."

"How's he been?" Amanda said.

Lessie turned to Art. "Your regular run-of-the-mill zombie. He's been a mouth breather since I came."

Jim grinned. "Not a pretty picture. We should get a snap of him and show it to him later."

"You're a mean son-of-a-bitch," Amanda said, then covered Melissa's ears. "Don't listen to us, honey. We're just tired and off our game."

Melissa smirked as she passed them and went to her dad. Standing next to the side table she rubbed his arm, the one stretched out with the catheter running into the vein. "Dad?"

Art did not respond.

"I don't get it. Shouldn't he be waking up?"

Jim nodded affirmation. "It's way past time. Didn't the doc say he could go home today? If he was doing better?"

"I'm going to find the doc see what she says." Amanda moved out of the room and left the three there looking at each other.

Lessie felt like going back to her seat but thought it would be rude for her to leave them and sit down. So, she stayed, feeling like she had a bright red pimple on the tip of her chin.

Amanda came back with the doc in tow, she explained to Amanda why Art was in the condition he seemed to be now. "The last blood test showed that drugs had been administered which knocking him out again. We didn't put any of the drugs into his system. We don't know how they got there. We do know a time frame for their introduction. Beyond that, we don't know how they got there."

"I think I might know," Lessie said.

They all turned to her.

"A woman dressed in scrubs came in here and spoke to Art just a few minutes before you all arrived. She asked Art a question. I couldn't get all of it, but she called him by name."

"What did she ask?"

"Like I said I could not hear her, but I heard 'Art,' then I couldn't hear until she said, 'ape?'

"Ape?" Jim studied the floor. "What could that mean?"

Tap, pause, tap, pause, tap. Amanda and Jim looked at each other.

Lessie stood taller and announced, "She's here."

Yvonne came into the room and gave them all a look that said she'd found them out and knew what they all were up too. She surveyed Art and looked back at them and over to Lessie. "Well I see the gentle giant returns. He seems whole and in one piece."

Lessie nodded toward the door, and Yvonne knew she wanted a little private talk. She gave her an almost nonexistent nod. They would meet outside this room soon.

Jim turned back to the doc, "Do you have any idea when he's going to be awake?"

Amanda asked, "What kind of drugs?"

The doc shook her head at Jim and turned to Amanda, "He was given a drug that stops convulsion. It causes amnesia, confusion, depression, hallucinations, headache, slurred speech, tremor, vertigo, agitation, anxiety, nightmares. I don't know how this man is going to come out of this. We won't know until he does and we can assess any brain damage the drugs may have done. Someone administered the most recent dose within the last four hours. We know from the blood draws. His blood draws before the last one showed him coming down off the drugs nicely. This last draw shows him back up. As I mentioned, we did not order any new drugs for him. Someone did this outside our protocol."

Amanda stepped over to Melissa and put her arms around her, holding her against her chest. Melissa allowed it for a little then pulled herself free. "Sorry honey, I just felt like I needed to protect you."

"I'm okay. I think I want my dad out of this hospital. Why can't he come home? We could have a nurse stay with him."

Amanda looked at Jim with an expression in her eyes the read "why not?" He looked back and gave her an "I don't know" shrug of his shoulders. Yvonne nodded and looked at Lessie who also nodded. They would be on watch at the Franklin residence.

"I don't think that's the best course of action for the patient. He needs care and our ER if necessary."

"My dad is not safe here. One of your doctors gave him more drugs. Which one?"

Jim looked at Melissa and said, "Yes, which one came into his room? Lessie, you saw her. What did she look like?"

Lessie shook her head. "Dark, short." Her hand went to her head and hovered over her own crown. "Kind of straight cut, boyish, Caucasian. Not sure of the height, she leaned over Art, put her hand on his chest."

"Did she have any rings, jewelry, tattoos?"

"No."

"Well, get the cell ready, we are circling in on her," Yvonne said.

Lessie looked at her and knew how unhappy Yvonne was at her lousy description of just about eighty percent of the people working here in the hospital.

"Mom!" Melissa squared her body making it clear she spoke to Amanda, "I want my dad moved home!"

Amanda stifled her shocked expression and the thought that she could lose her license. She stepped closer to Melissa, placing her arm over the girl's shoulders, and turned toward the doc. "What do we need to do?"

The doc shrugged her shoulders. "Call an ambulance, sign him out, and that's about it."

"Okay, let's do it!" Melissa said.

"Jim, you call, I'll sign him out," Amanda said.

"Amanda, how can you do that?" Jim whispered in her ear.

She whispered back, "Melissa's too young. I'm only the fiancé, but they don't need to know that." Amanda's eyes sparkled as she spoke to the doc, "Where do I sign?"

"Takes a little time to get the paperwork filled out and they can be brought here to you to sign. Then call the ambulance, and that's it," the Doctor said.

"Melissa and I will go home, get his room ready and come back probably before the papers arrive."

"No, I'm not leaving him. No one is getting anywhere near him." Melissa took a stand, and all of them looked at her. She would fight them all.

"Jim, you have a key?"

"To their house? Yes."

"Let's go." Amanda and Jim moved out of the room leaving Yvonne, Lessie, and Melissa looking at Art.

Yvonne caught Lessie's eye, and they moved toward the door into the hallway. "You didn't get anything more on this person?"

"I thought it was a nurse checking on Art. I realized it wasn't, but not soon enough. When I went to the door to see this person, the hallway was filled with people dressed just like her. I couldn't tell which one of them was her."

"Okay."

"What do you want to do?"

"Let me think."

Chapter Thirty-Six

3P.M. Sunday, October 22, 1995

"Jim," Amanda called out as she raced behind him to the Franklin front door. The bright red geraniums in the pots beside the door seemed welcoming, some loose leaves had fallen in the last wind burst nested in the corner of the cement just under the stucco by the door stop. Neither Jim or Amanda saw them as they rushed past.

"Yes?"

"I was just thinking, I'm not so sure this is the brightest idea I've ever had. Bringing Art home when he can't even help himself."

"I know." Jim slipped the key into the lock, and they listened to the bolt glide. He looked at her. "Melissa wants him home, and I think we have to do 'that', whatever 'that' means."

"It means an around the clock nurse."

"You mean," he opened the door, and they walked inside, "a registered nurse?"

She slung her purse on to the table in the foyer. "Yeah, I don't know how to take care of an unconscious man. Do you?"

They started for the upstairs and found Art's room. "I guess I could figure out what needs to be done," Jim said.

"I'm pretty sure I could not lift him. And I think there's lifting involved with someone who can't take care of themselves. Let's get these sheets changed." She pulled the covers back and grabbed a pillow, removing the pillowcase. "I'd better go find the linen closet and get another set for this bed." She left the room, and Jim continued pulling the old sheets off and piling them on the floor. Amanda came back and held a crème colored set. "This looks like what he'd use in here."

"Good, the dirty ones are on the floor."

"I see them. Run them down to the laundry will you while I put these on?"

"Sure." Jim leaned down and moaned. "You should see under his bed."

"What?"

"Loads of dust."

She leaned down and looked. "Good lord. We can't leave it that way. Better drag the vacuum in here as soon as this bed is made. Good thing it's high. I think I can get the vacuum under there." She smoothed the blanket over the bed and finished with the coverlet, turning the bed down as though waiting. "I'll go find the vacuum cleaner."

"I'll take these down. Shall I start them?"

"Yeah, why not."

"We'd better hurry. I want to sign those papers and get him home." They both left the bedroom, Jim, for the laundry and she for the vacuum cleaner. When Jim came back to the room she had pulled the side table away from the wall and had plugged the cord into the wall by the bed. It burst into energy and sucked the dust where she directed with great proficiency. "This won't take long."

Soon she reached for the plug and pulled it from the wall. "Jim, help me put that table back in place."

"Sure thing." He moved to pick up the table and stopped. "What's that?"

"What?"

"Something's by the leg of the bed, just a minute. Huh, I think this is the tape that Walt is looking for."

"Really? Should we get it to him?"

"No, not yet. First, let's get Art home. As soon as he wakes we'll see if he recognizes it." Jim put it down on the bedside table then lifted the table back into place.

"Didn't the cops look up here?"

"Yes."

"Then this can't be the tape. Those cops would have found it."

"Maybe and maybe not. It was hidden by the dust, and I just did see it. It might be the tape. Yeah, you're right. Once we get Art home, he can see it and maybe tell us what's on it. Or, we could listen to it and see for ourselves."

"We could."

"I think we are turning into investigators." Jim chuckled. "First thing we investigators should find is the player for that tape. Do you see one anywhere?"

They looked around and found themselves looking back at each other. "Probably in his office."

"Wonder why the tape isn't in his office. Why was it on the floor under his bed?"

"No point in going into that now. We'd better get back to the hospital."

"Let's get this show on the road."

Jim walked over to the table and picked up the tape. "I think I'm going to keep this just in case."

"Okay, lets' go."

They hurried downstairs and out on the porch and met the mailperson coming up the walk. Dressed in U.S. Post Office gray and blue shorts and shirt with a bag over her shoulder, she held out Art's mail and looked from Jim to Amanda, the expression saying, "You don't look like the people that live here." Then she caught Jim's grin and nodded. Someone she knew. "Have a good day."

"Thank you," Amanda said and shoved the mail into her purse. "At least we won't' have to deal with the mail when we come back."

Down the walk to the car, they banged the doors shut almost at the same time. Jim drove getting them to the hospital parking lot seven minutes later. "I'm a little nervous," Amanda said.

"I understand," Jim said. Taking her arm, they walked to the sidewalk, crossed the strip of grass and headed for the big glass door. Jim pressed it open, and they walked to the sign-in desk and identified themselves and were sent on their way upstairs.

In a few minutes, they were back in the room with the others. Yvonne stood at the end of the bed, one hand on the edge of the bed and one on her cane. Lessie stood beside her. Both were mum. They watched Art as Melissa leaned her head over the bed, her head on the pillow beside her dad's.

"Dad. You've got to wake up. I love you, Daddy. Can you hear me? Dad?"

Jim stepped over to Yvonne and asked if anyone had come into the room while they were gone. Yvonne shook her head. "Is this the tape Art showed you?" Jim brought it from his pocket. Her eyes narrowed, and she reached for the tape he held. Turning it over, she nodded.

"Yes, I think this is what he showed me. I think you should get it to Walt."

Jim understood and slipped the tape back in his pocket. "He hasn't' opened his eyes at all?"

"Nope."

A nurse came to the door, and they all turned to her, "The doctor just called and said she had signed off on this patient and the papers would be coming to us soon. I need to get him ready. You'll need to leave the room for a few minutes."

"No, I am not leaving. You can do whatever you have to do with me here." Melissa's determination filled the space with power. And the nurse worked around her. Art's hospital equipment that he was attached to was removed, one piece at a time. She dressed Art in a robe and placed slippers on his feet.

The nurse smiled as she worked with loving hands, making sure all that needed doing was done correctly. She grinned at Melissa as she passed by her and Melissa moved out of her way when needed. She finished and left the room.

Yvonne said she was going to go to the Franklin residence to make sure it was clear. She'd be there when they arrived. She offered Lessie to take the tape to Walt, if Jim wanted, and he agreed to give the tape to Lessie who dropped it into her bag as she slung it over her shoulder. They left, and Amanda, Jim, and Melissa studied each other, looked at the doorway, peered at their watches and waited for the papers. In a short time, two paramedics filled the door.

"We have a patient to transport?"

"Yes, my father. He's going home." Melissa said.

They looked at Art and saw he was out cold. A strange look passed their faces, but they said nothing.

Finally, the papers arrived, and Amanda signed and soon Art Franklin would be once again a free man. Unconscious, but free as a bird.

The men moved him from the bed he'd been occupying to their rolling gurney and all walked him to the elevator. Silently the door opened and they loaded up and dropped down to the ground floor. They went out a side door to the waiting ambulance. Jim said, "I've got my car in the main parking lot."

Amanda took control and said, "Melissa, you go with Jim. I am going with Art. "

Melissa complained, but Jim had her hand and pulled her along. "Come on, let's see if we can get home before they do."

They were running around the outside of the hospital, past bunkers of planting stations filled with greenery and sidewalks running along the outside edge. Jim led the way and Melissa stayed on his heels. Soon they were driving home, and Melissa turned her neck to see if the ambulance was following. Jim parked the car, and they were out when the ambulance turned the corner and came to a stop in the driveway. They removed Art from the back of the vehicle and wheeled him up the walk. Melissa had the front door open, and the men took Art inside. They made their way upstairs and put Art to bed. "It will be much better for this patient if you have a hospital bed downstairs. Until he's ambulatory."

"I didn't even think of that," Amanda said.

"My dad's going to be okay right where he is. I want him to wake up in his room."

Yvonne came into the room and set her cane against the wall. She took a chair by the window and sat.

"You going to stay?" Jim asked.

"Yes. Until Art wakes. It shouldn't be too long. I don't mind."

The front doorbell rang, and Jim trotted out of the room. When he returned, a nurse was with him. "The hospital sent Glenda over until you can hire someone."

"Hi," Glenda said, moving over to the patient and raising his arm to check his pressure.

Melissa came over to Jim and Amanda, "I don't want her here. I don't want anyone from the hospital."

Amanda took her by the elbow, "I understand honey, but we haven't called anyone in yet, and it might be until tomorrow before anyone can come. We need this help until then."

"I don't want anyone that might hurt him here. I don't know this person."

"We could call the hospital and find out if they did send her," Jim said.

"Yes, lets." Amanda and Jim left the room and went to the kitchen. They called the hospital and found out that no one from the hospital had been sent to help them. Alarm registered on both their faces and they started for the stairwell when the doorbell rang again. Jim ran to the door and opened it. Lessie came in, and then all hell broke loose upstairs. When the three hurried through the doorway, they saw Melissa with her arms around the nurse, fighting her. The nurse raised her arm up, the hand gripping a syringe dripping at the tip and waving around. Yvonne raised her cane and walloped the nurses' head. Lessie dove for the nurse's feet, wrapping her body around her legs and causing her to fall to the floor. Melissa held on tight. Yvonne gave the woman a couple more good smacks and Lessie worked her legs around the woman's body, squeezing Melissa out. A lot of moaning and groaning filled the space, and no one paid any attention to the patient.

"What the hell is going on?" Art said.

Chapter Thirty-Seven

5 P.M. Sunday, October 22, 1995

Melissa extricated herself from the nurse and Lessie who had suddenly wrapped a limb around the nurse's left leg. Melissa's hands landed widespread on the floor tripoding her with her right foot.

Up she came. "Dad." She was by his side in an instant. After staring at him, she turned to see what his eyes were plastered on. Together they looked on to the legs flying, the bodies bumping on the floor. There was huffing and puffing, but no one was going anyplace anytime soon. Yvonne's cane came down again and caught Lessie's shoulder, missing the nurse's head by five inches.

"Hey! Watch it!" Lessie said, heaving a heavy breath.

"Well, get out of the way!" Yvonne said as she maneuvered to smack the woman again.

"You get out of the way." Lessie's hand slipped around the woman's waist, "Do I have to do everything?" She grunted with effort, "Will you call 9 1... groan... 1."

Yvonne headed over to the phone on the nightstand. Art watched her progress while he looked at Melissa and said, "What the hell is going on here?"

"We are trying to save your life. That's what's going on here." Yvonne said, her voice losing thunder as she reached for the dial. She punched in 911 and told the dispatch they needed assistance. She put the phone down and turned to the doorway. "Boy, that's service."

Walt stood there. "Hi." He said, grinning at Art.

He held up the tape. "Been looking for this tape. Been trying to get the information from you, but you've been rather tight-lipped the last day. Looks like we have this parrot killing case all tied up."

The nurse stopped struggling, and Lessie raised her own body up as she straddled the woman on the floor, pressing down on her back between the shoulder blades.

"Who have you there?" Walt asked Lessie.

"This is a nurse from the hospital. She was about to shove something into Art's arm. Melissa and I caught her doing it. The syringe is on the floor somewhere."

Walt shuffled into the room and said, "Maybe it's time for his medicine?"

Melissa joined in, "He's not getting any more medicine. Amanda and Jim are calling the hospital to be sure she's even supposed to be here. We haven't called anyone. She showed up and started shoving his robe sleeve up and had the syringe poised and ready. It didn't seem right then, and it's not right now."

Two men in blue trotted up the stairs and came into the room followed by Amanda and Jim rushing their words as they came. "She's not from the hospital. They don't know who she is."

Walt pointed to the nurse. "Cuff her."

Lessie got up and let them reach the nurse. They had her cuffed and on her feet.

"Read her the rights and book her," Walt said. He turned toward Art when they had her out of the room. "Well, my friend, are you up to answering some questions now?"

"Yeah, I guess so. My heads fuzzy, but I can try." Art worked at sitting up, and Melissa and Amanda pushed pillows to hold him. Nothing seemed to work, and he finally settled at a sitting reclining position. "Shoot."

Walt walked over to the chair and pushed it around the end of the bed and close to the end table by the bed. "What do you remember last?"

Art's eyes darted around searching for an answer, and he came up with nothing.

"That's okay, Art. I talked to the doctor that took care of you. She said you were given something that messed up your thinking. She said we'd have to wait and see how you would come out of this. So, whatever you can remember, it would be good to talk about it sooner than later.

Art nodded. "Can you give me a time frame?"

Walt swung his head side to side, "Guess from where you left your car?"

"Left my car?" Art's perplexed expression left nothing to the imagination.

"Do you remember when you were home last? What were you doing?" Walt asked, keeping his voice soft and slow as he prodded Art's faint memory.

Everyone in the room turned from Walt to Art like watching a tennis match. The tension in the room heightened.

Walt picked up on it and told them to wait downstairs. They filed out of the room. All except Melissa. Walt gave her a searing stare. She gave him one back, and for some reason, she dropped her contact and kissed her dad on the forehead.

"I'll be just outside the door."

Art smiled, an "'I understand" look on his face.' She walked away, and Walt's voice cut the sound of her footfalls. "You wait in the kitchen with the others."

Melissa stopped, her back ridged, something on the tip of her tongue, but she held it in, the tension built, then she resumed her descent into the kitchen.

Walt sat forward, placing his elbows on his knees. "Think. What's the last thing you did?"

Art let out a deep breath, "Walt, my minds a blank. I can't settle on anything. I am curious why everyone's in my room."

"What's the last day you remember?"

Art grinned, "Tuesday. And I was on my way to the doctor's office." Art looked down at his arm. "I didn't make that appointment, did I?"

Walt only shook his head.

"What day is this?"

Walt looked at his watch. "It's Saturday afternoon."

"Where have I been for four days?"

"That's what I need you to tell me."

Art's expression sobered, and he said, "Water's dripping. I remember, a plunk and a while before, plunk again." His eyes shifted back and forth as he thought. "I remember darkness. There's something else. A woman, and the name Rio."

Walt listened.

"What did you mean you have the parrot killing case all tied up?" Art asked.

"Well, your short-term memory seems to be functioning. You and Jim found a tape and a dead parrot in Jim's house. You brought the tape to me, and we listened to it. We both thought it was a play. Someone practicing so that the bird could learn to say the words. Well, Art, the bird must have witnessed the killing as it happened. The drama must have been so heightened that the bird paid attention. There's a body with two bullet holes waiting in the freezer, and we've just ID'd him as Richard O'Neill, aka Ri O."

"Rio?"

"Yeah."

"That name's been circling around in my mind, and I don't know the connection."

"He's our dead guy, and the tape, I listened to it again. Points the finger at someone by the name of Sway."

"Sway?"

"Yeah, it seems our Mr. O'Neill married Proanne Swaysey. They are still married according to public records."

"Where is this Sway person?"

"If I'm right we just hauled her out of here, and," Walt leaned down, his fingers grabbing the needle by the part just coming down out of the syringe, "I'll bet this mix was meant for you." Walt managed to drop it into a plastic bag he withdrew from his pocket.

"Why? Why do this to me?"

"We will know that as soon as Sway tells us."

"You think she's alive?"

"Oh, yeah. If I am right, we just booked the killer."

"That nurse that was here?"

"Yep. Now that I know you are among the living I am headed back downtown to have a little talk with her. I will call you if I get anything this afternoon."

"There was a sweet smell that I remember, and I think I smelt it when she was here. If I'm right, that woman is the same woman in that dank, dark place, with the dripping water. I'm certain the smell is the same. You think she's the killer?"

"I'll check it out," Walt said.

Art felt relieved when everyone left him alone. He sat on the edge of the bed and looked toward his bathroom. Judging the distance as doable, Art slipped to the floor and felt watery legs. He held onto the edge of the bed all the way to the end of the mattress and looked at the side table where the chair belonged. He could make it if he tried. Art tightened his muscles and shakily made his way to the bathroom door. Hanging onto the door jamb, he steadied himself until he stood before the toilet. *That's the best feeling in the world.* He flushed and turned. A shower, oh how good that would feel.

Art studied his hands and wondered at the shaking. The legs held him up, and he walked to the shower door and opened it. He reached in and started the water. Art felt the towel hanging on the rack and knew he'd used it once. Confident he could not make it to the linen closet for another set he decided to use this one again. He fumbled with the robe and managed to get it untied and off his body. He had on one of those hospital gowns, and the thought passed his not-to-clear mind that he'd have to redress. If he could figure out how to get out of this contraption. Finally, the soft cloth fell away, and he stepped into the shower. The water sprayed over his back and shoulders, Art placed his hands on the walls, closed his eyes, let his neck fall back, raised his face up and let the steam fill the space. Heaven. "Awe."

He jumped when Jim spoke, "Hey, you're among the living if you want a shower. Do you want to go back to bed, or do you want some clothes?"

"Clothes."

"Good, 'cause in honor of your being home we are having a BBQ out back by the pool and I've been sent up to find out if you are hungry."

"I think I am. If you get out of here, I'll finish my shower and dry off."

"Okay, what do you want to wear?"

"Something easy. Shorts and a T would be good."

Walt sat across from Proanne Swaysey aka Glenda, the nurse, in the same room Amanda and Melissa used a night ago. They'd been together in this space for three and a half hours, and he smelt that sweet dead roses scent Art described. One of those scents you want to exit from. Like the smell of death. He observed her as she spoke.

"We took over the house, I don't know for sure, about a year ago, maybe more. We knew we had to make our living there impossible to find because they would have killed us both if they found us. Rio wouldn't stop gambling. He said that he had, but he'd be gone for a long time, and I knew. When Rio came back, he'd been gambling again. If I didn't kill him myself, I would probably be dead in a short time. There was no place to go. This was our last chance, and he blew it."

"You took over the house and dug out the cellar?"

"No, the cellar was that way, we just made the walls and doorways for our convenience."

"You are ready to give us a statement?"

Her dead eyes bore into Walt's. "For the protection you said I would have."

The chair scooted back, and Walt hauled himself up. "It'll be just a few minutes." Walt walked out of the room and got a pad of paper and a pen and pencil, the tip sharp, just the way he liked them. A grin played across his face. He'd done this one alone and without help and he loved the feeling. Holding onto the doorknob, he made his face stern, turned the knob and walked into the room. The woman seemed smaller, as though the life had drained out of her.

Walt placed the pad on the small table and pushed it toward her. He set the pen and pencil side by side within her reach, and then he sat. Saying nothing, he watched as she pulled the pad closer, and listened to the scratching of the soft lead. When she finished, she placed the pencil over the pad and pushed it away from her. She did not look up at Walt.

He pulled the pad toward him, checked to see that the information stayed the same and that it was dated and appropriately signed by her. Walt checked his watch and noted the time and placed his initials. "I'll have this typed up, and then you can sign it and we'll be done."

Walt stood, stepped out the door carrying the pad, the pen, and pencil. He nodded to the officer waiting outside that he'd be right back. The man acknowledged.

Walt came back with the statement typed out and ready to go. He went into the room, and when he exited he bobbed his head to the officer that he could take over.

Walt grinned again and looked around the department. *How sweet it is when things come together. He couldn't wait to tell Art.*

The sweet smell told Walt where to head.
"Hey. Come on, join us."

Walt nodded to Jim, "Thanks. BBQ? He took the plate Jim offered and filled it with corn on the cob, beans and ribs. "Where did you get these?" he said, biting into the pork smothered with sauce.

"I went to the store and bought them," Jim said.

"Boy, this is good." He slipped the manila folder on the table and pushed it toward Art.

Art eyed the envelope from the time Walt walked from the gate to the table by the pool.

Art's hand reached and brought the envelope up and waved it. His mustache twitched. "That was fast."

"Sway waived her rights to an attorney." Walt slathered butter over his ear of corn and raised it for all to see just before biting down on the fat end.

Art opened the manila envelope and slipped the typed pages out, noticing that they had a signature and a date and time stamp. He grinned as he brought the pages before him and adjusted his glasses. The grin faded as he read: 'I, Proanne Swaysey, killed my husband, Richard O'Neill, by shooting him on October 11th, 1995. I shot him two times in our home at 2638 S. Roselyn Road, Lodi CA.'

Jim looked up. "That's my address!"

"They were living there the whole time," Walt said, wiping his mouth with the paper towel napkin Amanda handed him.

"Butter's dripped all down your shirt," she said as Walt took the towel from Amanda.

"That's creepy," Melissa said putting a bone on her plate, "I can't imagine someone living in my house and I don't know about it."

Walt continued, "They evidently got into a row in the turret room, and that's where they had the bird's cage."

"Why kill him?" Melissa asked.

"According to this she didn't like the way he spent their money, seems Rio gambled."

"On the horses," Walt said, pulling the end pieces out of the corn cob and laying them on the table beside his plate. "They were in hiding because of his gambling debt, and according to her, he couldn't stop. They had moved from state to state and had nowhere else to go. If she didn't kill him someone else would, and her too. So, she figured she had to off him to live."

"And the parrot, how does the bird figure in this?"

"Aw, it wouldn't stop squealing. It was her bird, and they had taken it with them wherever they went.

Those creatures are smart and can copy what they hear. I don't know how they do it, but evidently the bird kept saying the words and Sway had to shut it up, and she put its body in the drawer so she could bury it later. She made the recording trying to get Rio to say he was the one who owed the money not her. He wouldn't do it I guess, and so she killed him. Why she didn't get rid of the bird and the tape is beyond me.

For the size of her she's a strong woman. She managed to get Rio's body to the lake and dump it in the water. And, Art's...."

"Me?"

Walt nodded, "Yes, she moved you into the basement area of Jim's house. That's where she kept you because she was trying to get you to tell her where the tape was. She wanted to get it back and get rid of it and you. Sway didn't get any useful information. I wonder if she knew that what she was giving you would make your mind fuzzy and you wouldn't remember anything."

"So," Jim said, "this Sway knew Art had the tape. She watched everything from her vantage point. God, I've got to demo that place to the ground and build it back up."

"Well, good people, I enjoyed the BBQ, but I've got to get back to the department." Walt stood, grabbed the manila envelope and patted Art's shoulder. "I am glad to see you, my friend."

"I am glad to see you."

Walt headed for the gate, and Jim and Melissa joined him.

Amanda pulled the foods together and made them ready for returning to the kitchen. She piled the paper plates together and gathered the utensils.

"Hey, you going to ignore me for very much longer, I'll go get me another beautiful blond."

She slid into his lap and lovingly caressed his jawline. "I could never ignore you, my love." Her hand brushed his hair back from his forehead. "The gentle giant returns."

His grin widened as his arm went around her waist and he snuggled close. She smelled so good, with that same fragrance he'd come to associate with her. "Who is the gentle giant?"

"Why, you are! Yvonne named you that at the hospital. It fits you."

They stayed that way for a long time, finally adjusting their bodies so that they were both looking at the river. The afternoon sun was sliding down and getting ready to array the evening with reds and blues mixed with vibrant oranges. But, now the trees were backlit and glowing. The sunlight managed to slice through the foliage, shafting onto the river, causing flashes to glinting like diamonds. The day was fading fast.

He kissed her head and felt the soft hairs on his lips. He cherished every one of them. How lucky a man was he to be holding this person in his arm and his heart.

The long silence ended when they both thought of something to say at the same time. The lovers laughed.

"You were thinking the same thing?"

"Yeah, I was."

THE GENTLE GIANT RETURNS

The gate opened, and as it did the flood lights illuminated the yard, and they turned at the sound the gate made. Jim and Melissa came carrying Daisy. She wiggled in Melissa's arms, and she let her down. Daisy raced across the yard and jumped against Art's leg.

He let her up and said, "My, but aren't you pretty." His hand felt the purple bow attached to her collar, he noticed her white hair now perfectly brushed out. "You took her to the groomers?" His expression said, "Without my approval!"

"What you don't know Art, is that it was Daisy that saved your life. She took me to you, and she wouldn't let up until I found you."

Art brought his eyes from Jim to the pup, "She did that?"

"Yes."

He looked into Amanda's eyes and saw "Yes." He looked at Melissa and she was so pleased. Daisy cuddled close to his chest and stretched her hind legs allowing her head to snuggle against his jaw line. After a moment he felt her warm tongue work his jaw. It felt good and he didn't protest. Instead, his eyes softened, a smile spread over his face and he said, "Well, it seems I have three special girls to look after."

THE END

SOMETIMES LOVES JUST MURDER

Chapter 1

Saturday, November 11, 1995

The clandestine woman ran, glancing furtively around and to the sides, but rarely to the rear. The cop in him spied a wild look in her eyes saying, without words, she was in trouble. As a semi Detective of Homicide for the Lodi Police Department, Arthur Franklin was immediately drawn in. He believed she didn't know he'd picked up on her, so there remained a discreet distance between them. Madam X, he'd call her that for now, fled, but from what? All Art could think of was if they kept moving as they were he'd soon be out of breath.

Her hair mesmerized him, swaying as it did, the different colors vivid in their contrast with streaked highlights of honey and gold, settling into waves of chocolate. It reminded him of his daughter, Melissa, when she had hair down to her waist. Only Melissa's hung straight, and this woman's hair waved and curled at the tips almost to her hips.

Madam X was a small woman by most statures, but curvy in all the right places. Her manner of dress spoke of a modest income and a classic style. Dark navy-blue pants and shirt with white piping looked stunning.

Noticing the way, the Grape Festival Grounds were laid out for this car show, and artwork event made him realize the need to be extra careful. His previously injured arm was the reason he was off work on disability and considered himself a semi-detective ached as he ran. Art clenched his teeth and pushed through the pain with each footfall. If he weren't careful, he would be bumping into not only the event throng but antique and classic cars, and Art knew their owners would not be happy with his handprint on their pristine paint jobs.

On the other hand, he needed two things in his life. Some excitement, and to blend in with the surroundings. These cars were perfect for hiding behind. He could stop on a dime and survey the closest vehicle and be one of the multitudes if the woman caught him in her field of view. On he jogged, feeling euphoria wash over him. At the same time, a tightening of the groin muscles as they protested each stretch made him admit, he was out of shape.

Somewhere in the back of his mind, he knew as happy as he felt was equal to how miserable he'd feel tomorrow. Today, it didn't matter. Art had to stay on the edge of things until he knew the who, what, where, and why of this unfolding small-town mystery. He was a happy man.

Art surmised the green sling trapping his left arm made his movements awkward, and he looked like an idiot. And anyone with an acute observance could figure out what was going on. He didn't care. Art felt sick and tired of the crap which had taken over his life for the last eleven months. He rolled his eyes as he admitted it.

Keeping about fifteen feet between them, Art slowed to a stop, dropped his head in the direction of a bright yellow Chevrolet Camaro, craftily slicing his eyes her direction he breathed heavily.

"Dad!"

Art's head swiveled without him willing it, at his sixteen-year old's call. "Melissa, hi. I thought you were with Amanda at the Art Museum?"

"I am. Amanda's found something, and she wants to show it to you. She doesn't want anyone else to get it, so she's staying right by it. "Why are you out of breath?"

"No reason."

Melissa studied him crinkling her forehead between her eyes. "Come on."

Torn? You bet. His eyes sailed back where he'd last seen Madam X by the stately Bentley. On tip-toes, all he saw was the chrome bumper gleaming and the head lights bordered off by the rope.

He had to go with Melissa and see this something, while his heart remained with the hot pursuit. He studied the cars parked close by and the ones further down the line, such beauties everyone. He looked behind the vehicles at the groups of people standing around.

"Dad!"

Madam X didn't seem to be anywhere. His shoulders dropped, the kid in him felt like a deflating balloon. Damn. Art had broken surveillance. His turning away to Melissa allowed enough time for the woman to disappear. A swear word surfaced, and he snuffed it. Well, why not say it? The world owed him. No! That's not right. The world isn't fair. He knew. Well crap!

"Dad, come on." She reached her hand out to him, the gold bracelets glistened in the sunshine. A welcoming smile crossed her face and the love in her eyes about floored Art. Somehow, he knew she didn't want him to be too far away. They'd almost lost each other twice, and yet it bothered her. He understood she knew in his line of work he ran into sick people all the time. They'd agreed, some time ago, Art seemed to be a magnet for them.

He gave Melissa his full attention. "Okay." They turned away from the path of the woman in blue, and headed back down the line of cars and turned along a roped area to the building with its doors standing open. A crowd of people milled just inside the doorway as Melissa and he worked their way around and past them.

Somewhere within the maze of freestanding walls and in the growing roar of conversations, Amanda waited. When Art and Melissa made their way through to her, he could see why she held her place. Two ducks, beaks together, about three feet high and sculpted to look life-like sought a new home. By the look on her face, they had found one.

He smiled and kissed her on her soft cheek taking in the aroma of violets from her shampooed hair. His mind went immediately to the day she'd blindfolded him and taken him for lunch at the farm with the lake and two mallard ducks. Amanda had said those ducks were lovers, like them. "Mutt and Jeff from our lunch at your friend's place in the country."

"Jan's." Yes. You remembered." Her grin could not contain the joy she felt, and it caught him up.

"How could I forget? Let's get it," he said.

"Oh, lets." She nodded to someone.

Art glanced, but the sea of bodies around swallowed up whoever she beckoned.

In a moment, a heavy-set woman arrived. "You've decided to take it home?" she said to Amanda.

"We have."

Art reached for his wallet.

The woman's cheeks blushed as her eyes sparkled and she unclipped her pen and wrote the sale up. "I enjoyed making this piece. It's got a story behind it, and maybe I'll tell you someday."

Art swelled with pride looking at his redheaded sixteen-year-old daughter, and his soon to be bride, the beautiful blonde shrink, Amanda Burtoni. Today they were operating as a family unit and acquiring their first memory piece together.

"How are we going to get it home?" Melissa asked looking at him to Amanda.

"We deliver!" the woman said.

That settled, Art took two steps away and made a quick return kissing both on their right cheeks as he said he wanted to go back to the cars. They both nodded and took the money he offered for the purchase. Art backed up and flowed back into the horde, feeling giddy and back on the hunt.

Where was the woman in blue?

The sun blinded him as soon as he stepped outside, and he put his hand up to shield his view. Everything swam as he focused and the glint off the sea of chrome and polished paint jobs didn't help. He sought her in every place and every group. She didn't appear anywhere. Art returned to the site Melissa intercepted him and found those Bentley headlights.

She wasn't anywhere.

Art momentarily accepted he'd probably would not ever see her again. Never learn what the excitement had been about. The sharp disappointment stabbed him like he had the right to know. Who was Madam X and why so scared?

His likeness mirrored in the window of one of the cars. The medical sling rode his blue shirt up at the collar making the whole appearance unsettled. Unprofessional. He got the shirt and sling under control, Art lifted the sling over his shirt and set it back in place, so the buttons on his blue shirt front were not caught up. All this led him to check his red hair and draw his hand through to settle the waves. The favorite feature about Art, his mustache, appeared neatly combed and brought a grin of satisfied pleasure.

The pleasure driven away by pain transported his attention back to the darn sling. Amanda asked him to use it at the show, 'Someone might bump into you, and if they see the sling it might stop them,' she had warned.

Yeah, yeah, he thought, or he might bump into someone. Satisfied with his appearance Art allowed his mind to switch back to the damsel in distress.

The woman's hair, was it a wig? It seemed so perfect. He couldn't let the intrigue go. Where was she? It became a struggle to bring his attention back to the cars.

He could see himself sitting behind the steering wheel of any one of these vehicles. Maybe when retired he'd join the car club. Art stepped next to the Bentley and read the placard in the front window, "Bentley, A Continental Flying Spur, color: Stormy grey, owned and displayed by; Jerry and Ruthi Heminger, Lodi Ca." Art strolled to the open window on the rider's side and leaned down to look inside. The leather seats so luxurious he wanted to rub them. The dash of golden marble. As he observed the elegant beauty of the manufactured car, the side mirror caught blue as it flashed by followed closely by the flip of hair.

Art reacted. Drew himself back from the car and raced to the rear of the English carriage and looked to the right. She must have just gone that direction. It must be the same woman.

Art stalked along the lane of cars peering around every curve every bumper and stopped facing a bright red 1962 Studebaker Gran Turismo. With dual headlights and squared body lines. His eyes narrowed as the young woman in blue jerked open the door and jumped into the driver's seat and slid down, as though to drop out of sight.

Art peered around. No one seemed to be interested in her, a grin spread across his face, the game was back on. Was she in real trouble as the expression in her eyes first told him? Or was this a joke she played on someone? Please, Lord, don't let it be me.

As he stood admiring the closed door concealing her body from sight, his hand raised a bit in preparation to reach for the handle instead he paused. His concentration dropped from the squared off driver's side window to the door panel with its chrome sweep from front fender to back. It broke the reflection into sections of the fleeing people.

"What the…?" he said as he turned.

Screaming began. Someone yelled, "Hey!"

When he looked back at the Studebaker, he saw how the shiny red paint mirrored a speeding Mercury Cougar. One who's engine roared, and twin front grills loomed like flaring nostrils. One that, if it kept coming at speed it would T-bone and sandwich Art between the two vehicles. This became real to him in an instant. It was happening! No more mystery, someone was after Madam X. intending to do bodily harm. She did need a shining knight to her rescue. Will this knight in a green sling and rusting armor be around to save her? At the rate the cars' approaching, whos going to rescue the shining knight? It would have to be him.

The distance between the Cougar and the Studebaker shortened considerably. Art let out a grunting sound with his exertion and pushed hard with his foot leaping clear. He hoped he'd guessed right as the air pressure from the approaching missile brushed his body.

Seconds later half the people heard the crash as real metal met and ground into real metal. The festive music filling the area was wholly drowned out by the screams of terrified people.

Slowly it all came to quiet bringing the melody at odds with the mood.

Dumbfounded people gathered around asking each other. "What just happened?" Until someone yelled. "Is anyone hurt?"

Art picked himself up, held his hurt arm at the elbow and made his way to the Studebaker's far side.

The door hung open, Madam X gone.

He came around the car and headed for the Cougar's door. A woman slumped over the steering wheel groaned. He pushed the brown hair from her neck. Her pulse beat fast.

Art turned and raised his hand to the gathering surrounding him. "Back up please, we need to make a path." He put his arm around Amanda feeling her warmth as she pushed through the crowd closest to him and reached his side. "Where's Mel?"

"She's with the ducks, I heard the crash and had to make sure you were okay."

"I am." He looked lovingly into her eyes, then spoke into his cell. "This is Arthur Franklin, I am reporting a vehicular accident involving one injury inside the Grape Festival Grounds. We need police and ambulance assistance."

"How come I am not surprised you're right in the middle of this?" Amanda said.

Enjoy these other novels ...
FROM PYNHAVYN PRESS

Funeral Singer Series – Paranormal/ Urban Fantasy

By Lillian I Wolfe

Music is a passion for Gillian Foster, a struggling musician with dreams of success. When an accident bestows a paranormal talent, her whole life takes an unexpected turn. Getting gigs as a funeral singer, she finds her conscious-self transported to an interim cemetery where she can speak to the recently departed while she is singing. Somehow, she is bound to help the spirit to complete any unfinished business.

But more than departed spirits haunt the transitional plane and they pose a threat to not only the souls in transit, but those still living as well. And they've identified Gillian as a danger. She's one soul against hundreds and she needs help.

Can she find others like her and rally enough to stop the spread of evil that can take everyone she loves?

The *Funeral Singer* series explores the overall theme as each thriller takes Gillian deeper into danger as she tries to help the departed souls cross to safety on the next ethereal plane.

Available to read now:
>*A Song for Marielle*
>*A Song for Menafee*
>*A Song of Betrayal*
>*A Song of Forgiveness*

Coming October 22, 2018: *A Song of Redemption*

O'Ceagan's Legacy: Book 1 (O'Ceagan Saga)
by Lillian I Wolfe (Sci-Fi Fantasy Adventure)

Trained by her grandfather to command, Grania O'Ceagan expects to one day inherit the family's space freighter, but first she must prove herself worthy to be captain. Her ambitious brother Liam is nipping at her heels and wants a ship as well.

On the return trip from Earth to their home world, they take on two unplanned passengers and find themselves facing a disaster that could destroy everything. Can Grania muster her crew and apply all she's learned to save her ship and crew from impending destruction?

For Eleven Million Reasons (The Franklin Logs)

by M.L. Weatherington - Police Mystery

If you think that winning the lottery is a dream come true, you need to read the possible dark side of publicized sudden wealth. In: *For Eleven Million Reasons*, mystery author M. L. Weatherington takes you on a suspenseful ride of murder and intrigue as Lt. Arthur Franklin pursues a killer. Don't miss this thrill ride of a first novel.

Sideswiped! (The Franklin Logs)

by M.L. Weatherington - Police Mystery

Picking up from the first book, Lt. Arthur Franklin of the Lodi Police Department finds himself suffering from doubt and uncertainty as he recuperates from the injury suffered in his last case–the one that nearly took his daughter's life. Melissa has retreated more than Art, who has been seeing a psychiatrist, Amanda Burton, a stunning woman and Art is undeniably attracted.

Meanwhile, a new murder has hit the streets of Lodi. Even though Art is on leave, his partner, Walt, wants to get his input on the case. With few clues to help them, it's a real puzzler. As things begin to escalate, Art is pulled into more than one mystery. Can Art help Walt solve the murder and how does it tie in with a mysterious stalker at his house?

Bitter Vintage

by Riona Kelly - Suspense Romance

When the heir to the Claremont Vineyards in Northern California is killed in an accident, his sister Martinique returns home for the funeral. She finds her father reclusive and odd, her estranged half-sister in residence, and a mysterious person skulking around the property. As she learns more about her brother's death, she is convinced there is more to the story and is determined to learn the truth. But can she prove it?

Bitter Vintage brings the suspense of treachery, greed, and ambition along with romance and betrayal as the story unfolds against the California vineyards of the Napa-Sonoma region and the migrant workers' struggle for fair wages in 1964.

Echoes of the Past

By Riona Kelly – Suspense Romance

A picture-perfect morning. A dead woman washed onto the beach.

Kathleen Donoghue's summer research trip to Wales turns upside down in that horrible moment when she finds the body. Without warning, the intrigue surrounding the victim sucks her into an eddy of unanswered questions. Who was she? How did she come to be washed ashore? Was it murder?

Alpha's Song (Les Loups-Garous)

by Angelina Fasano- YA Urban Fantasy

In a quiet little Kennington, Massachusetts, dark secrets abound and some are buried deeper than others. Mysterious club owner Daniel Hawthorne keeps them close to his heart.

Following the devastating death of her mother, Christa Ellsworth never expected to return to the town where she grew up, but five years later, she finds herself dragged back to the scene of her family's tragedy. Christa's plan to finish high school unnoticed comes to a halt following a chance encounter with the devastatingly handsome club owner she can't get out of her head. She begins to uncover the extraordinary truth about the town she grew up in and an unusual birthright that is now hers. Can she handle it?

Beta Rising (Les Loups-Garous)

By Angelina Fasano – YA Urban Fantasy

Continuing the story of from *Alpha's Song,* Christa finds her status as True Alpha challenged by an unexpected rogue pack.

Releasing in October 2018

Author Page

I have had such fun writing these stories and getting to know the characters as each one takes control of their lives. There was once in these words I've written that the character wanted to do something different from what I had planned. It set me back for a while as I contemplated it. Can you imagine how shocked I felt when I realized that the character was right and the story considerably better for the input.

Writing is a process and sometimes a painful one. During this one I moved, lost one of my dogs, and took on a new lifestyle.

Enjoy, I took pleasure in the writing.

M.L. Weatherington

Contacts: Blog: MLWeatheringtonauthor.com
E-mail: Weatheringtonmary@gmail.com

Reviews

Nona Wimsatt:

I have enjoyed the first book (FOR ELEVEN MILLION REASONS) so I have read it twice and now my baby sister Phyllis is reading it and she is having the same reaction as I. Can't put it down!! You go lady you are the Tops!

Cami E Ferry

Happy Friendversary, Amazing Gorgeous Talented Awesome Inspirational Mary!! From being a famous murder mystery novelist to being a famous murder mystery actress to being the all-around wonderful person you are and so much more...you are truly one of the most inspiring women I have ever met and I am so thankful, blessed, privileged, and honored to call you Friend...feels more like Family!! Love you and hope you will work with us at IMT again very soon!!

www.ingramcontent.com/pod-product-compliance
Lightning Source LLC
Chambersburg PA
CBHW071148170626

46809CB00002B/819